CLAIMING CAMILLE

About the Author

Louise McBain lives with her family and pets in Washington, DC.

CLAIMING CAMILLE

LOUISE MCBAIN

BELLA
BOOKS
2020

Bella Books, Inc.
P.O. Box 10543
Tallahassee, FL 32302

Printed in the United States of America on acid-free paper.

First Bella Books Edition 2020

Editor: Cath Walker
Cover Designer: Kayla Mancuso

ISBN: 978-1-64247-121-2

Acknowledgments

Writing this story would not have been possible without the love and support of my family and friends. Aside from copious grammatical assistance, they provided a fun, safe place for me to create. I cannot thank them enough for all they have done, and continue to do, to help me realize my dreams.

CHAPTER ONE

Shoop

Kicking cats away from the front door, Camille Robbins answered the bell. *Thank God the physical therapist was on time.* If the woman was as capable as the agency had promised, Camille could transition her father's care and be at the office by eight thirty a.m. It was two hours later than she wanted to arrive, but there was no avoiding the disruption in her schedule. She bit her lip. Any other day being late to work wouldn't be an issue. But this was her first time back in the Washington, DC office since transferring to San Francisco nearly eight years ago. She'd hoped to have more time to acclimate before the workday began.

She pulled open the front door, and a flash of fur to the left told her one of the cats was making a break for daylight. She moved to block it with the low heel of her shoe, but wasn't quick enough. The determined feline slipped through her legs and might have been two blocks down the street if a woman dressed in a chic white tracksuit hadn't hit it with her purse. Swinging the gorgeous patent leather handbag with impressive precision, she knocked the cat squarely back into the house.

"Thank you so much," Camille stammered.

The woman nodded as if this were a completely normal occurrence and offered Camille a crisp white envelope. "I am Martina. I think you are expecting me."

"Yes, please, come in." Camille stepped aside to let the woman enter and almost stumbled over the thwarted escapee.

"Khloe, stop!" she scolded the orange tabby. Two more felines joined the runner, and the trio began chasing each other around the entrance hall. Martina's face registered benign surprise but she didn't comment. Camille cursed her luck. *Great first impression, stellar.*

The cat situation was slightly mortifying, and not easily explained. One day, about a year after Camille's mother died, her father had gone for a walk and come back with five cats. A mother and four kittens he had, of course, named them after the Kardashians: Kourtney, Kim, Khloe, Kris and Rob. Camille still wasn't sure how he'd pulled it off. When her assistant Cory had adopted a cat, there'd been more paperwork than when Camille had purchased her townhouse. There had also been weeks of home visits, reference checks, and the menacing possibility of future contact. Cat adoption professionals did not play around.

Camille knew Joe Robbins hadn't obtained the Kardashians through such strict channels. But when she'd questioned him, the normally unflappable media studies professor had been indignant. He'd surprised Camille by raising his voice, loudly announcing that he'd missed out on having cats his entire adult life. Camille's mother had been allergic and had persuaded him to keep fish instead. *Fish! They were so much work and gave nothing back. Nothing!* In the end, Camille had been supportive. If her father wanted cats, he should have cats. Why he needed five cats simultaneously was a question for another time.

One of the Kardashian sisters, perhaps Kim, left the game and moved over to rub against Martina's ankle.

"I'm sorry," Camille apologized, noticing with embarrassment that cat hair now clung to the physical therapist's white pants.

"It is nothing." Martina smiled and her entire face changed as fine lines around her eyes and mouth softened her imperious beauty.

Camille couldn't help but smile in return. "Thank you. The cats belong to my father." She nodded toward a pair of paneled doors to the left of the foyer. "There's a futon in his office. The stairs are difficult to manage with his injuries, so he's sleeping in there."

"That is best. He has a bathroom downstairs too?"

"Yes, it's just here." Camille pointed to a door further down the hall. The Woodley Park home was a standard colonial with three upstairs bedrooms and a finished basement. Her parents had bought it more than thirty years ago when her mother, Mary, had been pregnant with Camille. The modest brick house was the only place Camille had ever truly considered home.

"The agency filled me in on your father's case. How is he feeling today?" Martina gave her crinkly smile again, and Camille relaxed even further.

"Better than yesterday, I think. I just gave him breakfast, and his morning meds. The painkillers may be making him a bit loopy though. He's acting a little silly...well, sillier than usual."

Martina nodded, as if this were to be expected. "That is good news."

"Really? He's supposed to be high?"

"It tells us his body is mending. He doesn't need so much medicine for pain so it goes to his head. I'll review the dosage with his doctor."

"Thank you."

"It is my job," Martina said simply. "I will also assess his mobility and get him started on some exercises to stop muscle atrophy."

"That sounds great."

"Shall I meet the patient?"

"Yes, follow me please."

"You are a very good daughter to care for your father."

"Thank you." Camille quashed a surge of guilt. She'd only agreed to come home because there'd been a break in her schedule. An age-discrimination suit had settled early leaving her unexpectedly free. Optimally, Camille would have used the time to work on her new townhouse—she'd yet to buy bedroom furniture or kitchen appliances—but five years had passed since she'd last been to DC. And her father had asked.

"He may be sleeping," Camille explained as she tapped the tall paneled door twice with her knuckles. There was no answer.

"Wake him gently."

Camille's absence hadn't been intentional. Life had just been busy. Camille's polite English father hadn't seemed to notice anyway. He'd seemed perfectly happy traveling to California a few times a year, staying in a hotel and calling it a relationship. She knocked again. This time, a bit louder.

"I'm alive!" came a muffled call from behind the doors. Camille smiled weakly.

Before her mother died eight years ago, Camille and her father had been close. She would have entered his room without knocking. But grief over Mary Robbins's death had driven a wedge between them. It was no one's fault. It wasn't that Camille's father wouldn't share his grief—he just didn't know how. Joe had mourned his wife privately, keeping a stoic public front while Camille had grieved openly. She'd stopped eating, sobbed endlessly, lost weight. Joe had given her a wide berth and a clean handkerchief, but never offered his shoulder. Therapy had moved Camille beyond resentment and into a place of understanding. She knew it would take time to reestablish a close relationship with her father, but she was trying, and things were getting better.

She rolled the door into the wall. "He doesn't usually nap this early. But as you said, it may be time to dial back the meds."

"How long have you been caring for him?"

"Just a few days. I wish I could do more. But my training is in law, not medicine."

Martina patted her arm. "He is lucky to have you."

Camille experienced another stab of guilt. "Thank you."

Joe Robbins had been suspiciously insistent that Camille come home to care for him. After three days in the house she'd understood why. It had very little to do with his convalescence and everything to do with his cats. The litter boxes were kept in the basement. Camille's childhood playroom, a sacred space that had borne witness to every stage of her life from finger painting to finger fucking, was now effectively a cat lavatory. It was awful. Steep stairs prevented Joe from performing the chore himself so Camille had been enlisted. She'd scooped the boxes exactly once since returning home and was not looking forward to doing it again.

The Kardashian sisters raced past them into Joe's office.

"I'm sorry about the cats." Camille watched Martina for a reaction. There was a chance she would bolt if she learned there were two more.

"Please, don't apologize. It only means your father has lots of room in his heart."

Though unintentional, the remark cut Camille to the quick. It galled her to think the emptiness in her father's heart was so vast that he'd had to fill it with cats. Tears threatened, and she felt Martina's warm hand on her arm.

"Is everything okay?"

"Yes, I'm sorry." Camille wiped at her eyes. "I don't know what's wrong with me."

"Please, let the tears come." With practiced care, Martina reached up and pulled Camille's hand away from her face, leaving behind a hint of floral perfume.

They entered Joe's office and Martina's eyes widened slightly at the elaborate floor-to-ceiling cat activity center dominating the room. Camille approached her father and laid a hand on the convertible futon he'd been sleeping on since his accident.

"Dad, Martina, your physical therapist, is here. She's going to get you started on some exercises."

"Good morning, Joe." Martina walked toward the futon. She was a voluptuous Italian woman in her mid-sixties, wearing an expensive-looking tracksuit with a fancy designer logo that Camille didn't recognize. Her salt-and-pepper hair, twisted into a neat chignon, was effortlessly elegant. Joe looked up from the *New York Times* and his bright green eyes, so much like Camille's, lit with obvious interest. Camille watched in horror as they dropped to Martina's ample bosom.

"*Buongiorno.*"

The meds were definitely affecting him.

"*Buongiorno*, Joe, is there anything you need?"

"I'd fancy a cuddle." He tried to execute a rakish smile, but his facial abrasions from the accident lent more menace than charm.

"Dad!" Camille squeaked, but Martina shook her head.

"You're not well enough for that. Also, I am too much woman."

"But what a way to go!" He giggled and again tried to smile. Camille felt sick.

A week prior, a texting Uber driver had knocked her father off his bicycle. He'd landed in a beautifully landscaped flower bed on Nebraska Avenue, suffering road burn, a broken femur, two cracked ribs and a moderate concussion. The prognosis was for a full recovery. Joe had been very lucky but the bicycle was now a tangled mess of tires and titanium, serving (at Joe's insistence) as a cautionary sculpture in the American University quad.

"But I am here to help you." Martina laid a hand on the nylon brace immobilizing his leg. "Tell me, how are you feeling today?"

"I falafel," he replied, and giggled again.

Martina looked quizzically at Camille.

"The man who hit him was ordering Lebanese takeout. 'I falafel' is his new favorite joke." Camille shook her head apologetically.

"But that is funny." Martina smiled. "And a good sign. Good humor is best for good healing."

Joe beamed like a first grader awarded a gold star.

Camille glanced at the mantel clock. If she took the Metro to Dupont Circle, she'd likely make it the office by eight thirty. The train would be crowded but it would be faster than walking. Martina read Camille's body language and shooed her toward the door.

"I think you have someplace to be?"

"Yes, actually. I'm on my way to work."

"Then go. Joe and I will have a nice morning. Right, Joe?"

"So very nice," her father said, staring at Martina's breasts again.

"Dad!"

"It's okay, Camille. We will sort out his medicine and then begin some exercises. Go to work."

"If you're sure?"

"I'm sure."

Ten minutes later, Camille was walking toward the Woodley Park Metro Station. The DC offices of Walker and Jenkins were in Dupont Circle, either a mile and a half walk or one train stop away. Today Camille would take the Metro. Striding briskly to the station, she took the opportunity to check in with Cory. It was obscenely early in California, but this morning Cory was at his mother's house in Atlanta and would be up drinking green tea and watching *The Today Show*. He was using the unexpected break as an opportunity for a home visit of his own. He answered the phone on the first ring and began scatter-shooting questions.

"How's the office? Have you seen Mia yet? Will you please FaceTime me so I can see what you're wearing?"

"Good morning to you too, Cory. How's your mom?"

"Mean and fat, just like always. I can't believe I'm wasting my vacation time here. Right now she's out buying ammunition for her BB gun so she can shoot squirrels off her bird feeder. Answer my questions, please."

"I'm not at the office yet."

There was a long pause. "Are you sick? Please tell me you wore the facemask I gave you for the plane. You never got a flu shot this year. Not even when that nurse came to the office."

"There wasn't time. But don't worry, I'm not sick. I'm just late."

"Oh."

Cory's confusion was understandable. Camille's early mornings were normally non-negotiable. It was a habit she'd started at the University of Virginia School of Law nearly ten years ago. Arriving two hours before the office workday began gave her two hours to get her bearings. She could do the pregame check of email, voice mail and caffeine. It was the difference between easing yourself into a lake and diving right in. Today she'd be forced to take the plunge.

It didn't matter too much, because Camille didn't have any pressing cases. On family leave, her schedule was clear and her time her own. She'd also capitalized on needing a temporary office at Walker and Jenkins DC branch for political reasons. The firm would announce the new partners in a few weeks. Being seen around the head office could only improve Camille's chances. She explained this strategy to Cory and then her reason for being late.

"Martina? Does she play tennis?"

Camille rolled her eyes but couldn't suppress a giggle. Cory was a whip-thin southern boy with a whip-sharp wit to match. He'd been Camille's legal assistant for nearly five years. "It wasn't on her resumé but I can ask her."

"Are you wearing the Prada suit from the sample sale?"

Camille looked down at the pencil skirt and high-waisted suit jacket he'd insisted she buy the month before.

"I am."

"Good girl. The green makes your eyes pop and the skirt makes your ass look like a work of art."

"Cory."

"It's true. The Pilates has paid off. Wait until that bitch *Mianderthal* sees you. She'll come sniffing back around. Just watch."

"Thanks. But that's not what I want. Not at all."

"I know. All you care about is making partner, your new townhouse, Pilates and…"

"You," Camille finished the sentence. "I care about you and that's enough."

"I care about you too, sweetie. Will you text me tonight? I'll be at the farm tomorrow and there's no cell service out there. Just chickens and Chinese checkers. Lord, help me."

"That actually sounds fun." Camille thought of Cory with his family and smiled. A thought occurred to her. "Will you please send Bobby my notes on the Frackit appeal before you go to the farm?"

Cory snorted. "You really think there's going to be an appeal?"

"I think we need to be prepared. Send Bobby the notes?"

"I already did."

"You're perfect."

"I really am."

Bobby Fry was one of several partners at Walker and Jenkins who gave Camille employment work. Earlier in Camille's career, her law practice had been less defined. She'd dabbled in insurance cases, commercial litigation, really anything a partner asked her to do. But since moving to San Francisco, she'd found a personal niche in employment law. Her last case had ended in very public success.

"You know that preparing for an appeal is a waste of time?"

"I don't know that."

"You beat the shit out of Skater Boy."

"Be that as it may."

Last month Camille had successfully defended a virtual gaming company in Silicon Valley from an age-discrimination suit brought by a twenty-nine-year-old celebrity coder named

Scotty Blalock, aka Skater Boy. Though neither federal nor California law protected workers under the age of forty from age discrimination, Skater Boy had filed suit anyway.

Then he'd written an op-ed in the *San Francisco Chronicle* lamenting the injustice of age-based bias. It had been a blatant publicity stunt but Camille had kept her eye on the ball. Arguing the illegitimacy of his claim, she'd filed a motion to dismiss, had her picture in the paper and won the case before it even went to trial. The positive result would not hurt her partnership chances.

"Did Bobby text back?" There was little chance Skater Boy would file a notice of appeal—the district court judge had been clear she thought the lawsuit frivolous—but Camille couldn't be too careful. The lawsuit, though unsuccessful, had garnered enough unwanted publicity for the software company. Bad press affected profit points.

"Bobby's on a yacht in Cabo celebrating with the Frackit CEO."

"Is that kid old enough to drink?"

"That's why they went to Mexico. Duh."

"Oh, yeah, duh."

Cory was Camille's closest confidante in San Francisco where, by design, her social life was almost nonexistent. She simply had no time. If Cory wasn't her assistant and also absolutely charming, it was doubtful he'd be in her life either. Camille found that she got the maximum return on her days if she didn't clutter them up with people. Personally, she made no claims on anyone and allowed none to be made on her. Yes, her life was devoid of intimacy but it was much safer this way. Camille was happy to admit this, though it drove her therapist to make long speeches about the important difference between self-realization and self-actualization.

Camille worked hard and saved her money. As a result, she'd achieved nearly all she'd set out to do. Six months ago, she'd closed on her townhouse and the partnership announcement was imminent. It lacked only the perfunctory vote at the annual partners' meeting, scheduled for later in the month. All Camille's dreams were coming true, but why wasn't she happier?

She arrived at Woodley Park station and walked down the massive escalator. She loved taking the train to work. It wasn't just the convenience—it was the energy. There was something electric about being caught up in the rush of a new workday. Camille had always reveled in the collective purpose and intent of the other passengers. When she was a little girl she'd imagined it powered the train.

Stepping off the escalator, she experienced a sense of emotional déjà-vu that left her rattled, though not surprised. This had been her route to work the summer she'd first met Mia. The sense memory of the location put her back there like it was yesterday. As commuters rushed past her, Camille took a moment for the highlight reel to play out and was gratified to feel only nostalgia rather than longing or regret. She was relieved. The trifecta of time, distance, and therapy had healed her broken heart. Mia was a defining relationship in Camille's life, but she no longer defined Camille.

The round lights lining the tracks began to blink, alerting those on the platform to an incoming train. Camille could hear the rumbling through the tunnel and moved with the crowd to position herself for boarding. The lights started blinking more quickly and the train barreled into view, the brakes squeaking in protest as the driver brought the cars to a halt. The doors opened, revealing a wall of people packed together like a bamboo forest. They locked eyes with the commuters on the platform. Camille felt the challenge in the air and rose to meet it.

One stop later, she exited the train at Dupont Circle and headed toward the behemoth escalator up to the street. Camille remembered that it had two hundred and ninety-one steps. The Woodley Park Station had an even higher stair count at three hundred and forty-two. She'd memorized the numbers in seventh grade, when her brain must have had a special adhesive. Also committed to memory were all her middle school friends' birthdays and the lyrics to Salt-N-Pepa's *Very Necessary* album.

Perhaps it was the spring air or being back in the city of her youth or maybe it was that "Shoop" had begun playing in her head, but Camille felt a surge of hope. Martina seemed like a good fit. Physical therapy would help Joe Robbins get back to scooping his own litter boxes very soon. Camille could go back to San Francisco with a clear conscious and a better relationship with her father.

She stepped onto the inside escalator and began walking up the moving staircase. "Shoop" pounded on her internal soundtrack. She nodded her head to the beat of the song as the lyrics played in her head. Camille had sung it in high school to psyche herself up before tennis matches. The first line always got her going.

Here I go! Here I go! Here I go, again!

Nodding to the beat, she continued her personal affirmations. There was every reason to feel good about herself. At thirty-five, she was poised to make partner in one of the country's top law firms. She owned a Victorian townhouse in San Francisco. She had her health, Cory to gossip with, a few investments and Val, a very nice woman who asked nothing of her beyond an occasional, very satisfying fuck.

It was the perfect arrangement. Val rented the basement apartment next door and traveled extensively. Every six weeks or so, she'd show up on Camille's doorstep with a bottle of pinot noir and a big, fat joint. Camille enjoyed the sweet release elicited from the talented fingers of her enigmatic neighbor but didn't worry if Val would remember her birthday. In fact, Val couldn't remember her birthday, because Camille had never told her the date.

Her quads began to burn as she pushed herself to continue the ascent. Dredging up more lyrics to the song, she lifted her legs to the beat.

I like what you do, when you do the voodoo that you do so well. Make me wanna Shoop!

She worked her body harder, not looking up for fear that if she saw the remaining distance, she'd get psyched-out and stop.

Camille didn't realize she was singing out loud, until she heard the words echoing down from above. Confused, she looked up into the smiling eyes of a woman moving toward her on the downward escalator. A very pretty woman who'd also chosen to walk the steps. A woman who was looking directly into Camille's eyes and singing.

CHAPTER TWO

Welcome to the Team

The managing partner personally escorted Camille to her temporary office at Walker and Jenkins. It was an excellent sign. The courtesy went well beyond Steve Benson's prescribed duties and sent Camille a clear message. The long-awaited partnership was on track. The venerable lion of the firm did not get out from behind his massive desk for just anyone. Camille was now considered a peer and thus deserving of peer treatment.

"How's the coffee?" he asked, squinting affably down at her. Camille smiled back noticing that what hair he had left was wrapped around his head like Caesar's crown.

"Good," she lied and pretended to sip the scalding rocket fuel.

"Best beans in the city," he informed her. She recognized the tone of a zealot and was careful not to offer an opinion. Sharing his special brew with her, as noxious as she found it, was another excellent sign. She was sure now that the partnership was a lock.

Gliding down the hallway, Camille felt almost weightless. She allowed it to sink in.

Making partner at a major law firm was a huge accomplishment. Camille's value lay in being a worker bee, her success attributable to long, hard hours and zero mistakes. It made for a boring life, but the endless slog of late nights and weekend work was about to pay off. Her mother would have been beyond proud. To become an equity partner, Camille would need to attract clients of her own, become a rainmaker. But that was the next rung on the ladder. Today she would enjoy her success.

"Congratulations on the Frackit dismissal," Benson said amiably. "I understand you're doing great work in California. Bobby Fry says you go the extra mile for the client. That's fantastic, Camille, fantastic. I had to remind Bobby that we trained you. I think he's worried we'll lure you back."

"Thanks, Steve," Camille said sincerely. The compliment meant a great deal. She had no desire to relocate to DC but it was nice to be considered. "But I'm only here a couple weeks to look after my dad."

"How's he doing?"

"He's much better. Thanks for loaning me the office."

"It's no problem." Benson stopped at a heavy wooden door at the end of the hallway, and pulled out a key card. "Beverly's out on maternity leave for the next six weeks. You got lucky. She's got the best office in the building. We're all very jealous." He opened the door and stood back for Camille to enter.

The first thing she noticed was the light. Looking over Massachusetts Avenue, the large corner office caught the morning sun. Camille could easily imagine why the other attorneys might be envious. Bright rays dropped in through a bay window on the east side, bouncing light across the room and washing everything in warmth. The effect was dazzling. Plaster on the frescoed ceiling looked white as bone. The beveled mirror above the mantel sparkled like water.

"This is stunning." Camille walked farther into the office, taking in the architectural details. The building was older than her townhouse, but it had the same feeling of permanence, of something built to last.

"The light is certainly beautiful," Benson replied dryly.

Camille wondered at his tone. It wasn't until she looked around a bit more that she began to understand. *Oh, dear.* Beverly Stanley liked baseball. She liked baseball a lot. The Washington Nationals in particular. Camille spun in a circle to take it all in. There was enough Nats swag in the room to host a pop-up sale.

"Beverly is a Nats fan," she said finally, causing Benson to laugh out loud. His tall frame shook with genuine mirth.

"They told me you were quick." He winked at Camille, who continued to gawk.

Every flat surface in the room was covered in Washington Nationals paraphernalia. It looked like an MLB gift shop. In addition to the mini ball caps and bobbleheads there were clocks and cups, snow globes and ashtrays. *Did people even smoke anymore?*

Rows of bobbleheads lined the two main levels of the fireplace's intricately carved mahogany mantel. On a higher tier, ceramic garden gnomes in Nationals uniforms stood stalwartly out of place in front of the hand-painted tiles. A giant eagle was propped against the hearth, along with what looked to Camille to be stuffed-animal US Presidents. Only Teddy Roosevelt looked happy, his face beaming in the spotlight. The rest suffered silently. Camille did not make eye contact with Lincoln, lest she embarrass them both.

"I'll leave you to start your day," Benson said, interrupting her thoughts.

"Okay, Steve. Thanks for walking me down." She wanted him to know the gesture had not gone unnoticed.

He gave her his politician's smile. "Not a problem."

The door closed and Camille put her laptop bag down on top of the Washington Nationals desk blotter. A brass plate next to the matching pen set identified the owner as Beverly Stanley, Nationals Fanatic. At least she was owning it.

Camille chided herself for being snarky. If anything, Beverly Stanley deserved her sympathy. Hadn't Camille seen firsthand how an interest could grow into a hobby and how a hobby could turn into an obsession?

Camille's mother had collected so many ornamental frogs that her father had special shelves built in the basement. By the time she'd died there'd been more than four hundred. Porcelain frogs, jade frogs, crystal frogs, carved wooden frogs, frogs made of dried pasta which Camille had glued together in elementary school. Like a biblical plague, they'd begun attaching themselves to Mary Robbins in early life, and by the time Camille was born, they'd colonized the entire house. Individually they were whimsical and fun. Taken together they were madness. *Amphibian delirium.*

Wow, Camille hadn't thought about the frogs in a long time. As far as she knew, they were still in the basement, awaiting the estate sale that would be their ultimate destiny.

Beverly Stanley, Nationals Fanatic, was at defcon-frog with the Washington Nationals. But professionally, it didn't seem to have hindered her success. Camille looked around the impressive corner office and made a mental note to check out a few games once her dad was feeling better.

There was a light tapping on the door and Camille's gut tightened. She hoped it wasn't Mia—not so soon. She'd worried that she might have to see her former lover eventually, but not now. Not when the day was going so well.

The knock sounded again, this time more insistent. Camille straightened her skirt and braced herself for the confrontation. A feeling of dread churned in her stomach next to Benson's high-octane coffee. Before she reached the door, it cracked open, revealing a far more welcome sight.

"Jenna the Antenna," Camille whispered reverently. Reaching out, she pulled a tiny woman through the doorway into an automatic hug. Detecting the familiar scents of patchouli and Juicy Fruit gum, she couldn't help but smile.

"Thank God you're here."

Jenna whipped her head from side to side, as if scanning the room for insurgents. Impulsively, Camille hugged her again. Closing the office door, she leaned against it and crossed her arms. "So, I hear you're a stuffy old lawyer now."

Jenna's oversized eyes widened even further with delight, but she nodded without smiling.

"And I hear you're a soon-to-be asshole partner."

Camille grinned, and they both said "Congratulations" at exactly the same time, and then "Jinx!"

Falling into chairs, they laughed at the improbability of the situation. Camille and Jenna had started on Mia's team on the same day, Camille as an associate attorney and Jenna as a paralegal and research assistant. Despite Jenna's subordinate position, a camaraderie had blossomed between the two young women. They'd hit it off immediately, sharing a mutual awe of Mia and an obsession with the giant sushi toro roll at the restaurant across the street.

Over time their connection had deepened and they'd become true confidantes. Jenna had been the only other person at the firm to know about Camille's affair with Mia. Camille had been a bridesmaid at Jenna's wedding. She'd traveled to the Bahamas with a plane full of Jenna's crazy relatives and toasted her friend and her new wife under a beautiful Caribbean sky.

They'd kept in touch through social media, so Camille was up on Jenna's life. She knew she and her wife Melissa had just moved outside the city to a house in the trendy northern Virginia neighborhood of Del Ray, and that they had a puppy. But Camille and Jenna hadn't had an intimate talk in years. Their personal contact had dwindled to birthday texts and likes on Instagram. Camille felt a stab of regret.

"So, how hard do you suck?" Jenna asked as if reading her mind.

"Jenna, I'm…" Camille began but her friend cut her off.

"A lazy bitch, who forgot all about the person who held her hair back when she puked up Jägermeister behind the dumpster at the 9:30 Club?" Jenna finished the sentence. Despite her words, her eyes flashed with the perfect combination of love and mischief. Camille felt a wave of nostalgia wash over her. How had she lost contact with Jenna?

"Yes, in fact, *I am* that lazy bitch," Camille agreed, and then leaned back in her chair to regard her old friend. It seemed miraculous, but their intimacy was instantly restored. As if just yesterday they'd shared a pitcher of margaritas at Lauriol Plaza.

"I thought that was you," Jenna replied, brown ringlets bouncing around her shoulders.

"And you, my dear," Camille said, "are a shameless whore who came to San Francisco, posted photos of yourself on social media and did not call me."

"It was my cousin's wedding!"

"You were shameless."

"You were lazy."

"We suck."

"We do."

"Well, you look stunning." Jenna fluttered a hand in Camille's direction. "You're all shiny, very California."

Camille blushed, but accepted the compliment with grace. She knew she looked different. Part of it was relentless Pilates, but the other part was just as Jenna had said. It was California. There was something about being in a place where everyone took care of themselves that had made her want to raise her game. The remedies had been pretty basic. She'd taken up exercise and stopped eating red meat and sugar. Camille had begun treating her own animal body as she would a beloved pet, and it showed. The margarita fat she'd acquired in college and law school had melted away like a redundant second skin. The body that had emerged was lithe and spare, angular in places where there'd been curves. But that wasn't all. She'd let her hair grow out of the preppy bob Mia had preferred. It now brushed past her shoulders. Today, the dark blond mass was piled on top of her head, secured in place with a tortoiseshell clip.

"And you look…" Camille considered the best adjective to describe Jenna's appearance. Camille had always thought her friend looked like the 1920's silent film actress Clara Bow. Her curly brown ringlets offset luminous brown eyes and a pouty little mouth. She was simply adorable. Jenna looked at her expectantly.

"I think you look exactly the same."

"The same? I just said you were stunning!"

"Well, you were stunning five years ago."

"True." Jenna rubbed her palms together. "Okay, let's spill some tea."

"What?" Camille looked at Jenna's empty hands. "We can't make a mess in here. I only have the office on loan. I would hate to break anything."

"*That* would be a travesty." Jenna picked up a Washington Nationals snow globe and gave it a vigorous shake. Red stars dropped over the tiny baseball player inside. "But I'm not talking about a Boston Tea Party, Camille. A spill-the-tea party is about gossip."

Camille shook her head. Her friend was not called Jenna the Antenna just because the words rhymed. The woman did not miss a trick. Not only did she have the best gaydar Camille had ever seen, but her nose for news was uncanny. She'd been an excellent research assistant before going back to law school.

"Do you have something you want to tell me?"

"There may be something of interest."

"Is it about Mia?"

"Who else?"

"Do I want to know?"

"I don't know, Cam-o-flage. You tell me?"

Camille cringed at the old nickname. It had been Jenna's gentle joke about the clandestine nature of Camille's relationship with Mia. She had also called her Double-O-Robbins, with the emphasis always on the O.

"Well forewarned is forearmed, and all that."

"Am I going into battle?"

"It is Mia we're talking about."

Camille closed her eyes. "Good point."

A loud knock interrupted their conversation and Camille started. Jenna was quick to reassure her. "Don't worry, girl. The dragon lady is not in the office today."

Camille blushed as relief flooded her body like a dose of Xanax. Though secure that Mia no longer had the power to control her, she was still apprehensive about seeing her again.

The knock sounded a second time, and Steve Benson ducked his head through the door. If he was surprised to find Jenna, he didn't show it. A natural politician, he acknowledged her warmly, then asked her about her cases, Melissa, and even the new house in Del Ray. Niceties over, he turned to Camille.

"Do you have a sec?"

There was only one answer to his question. "Sure."

He turned to Jenna. "I hope I'm not interrupting anything important."

"Nothing that won't keep." Jenna rose from the chair, and smirking at Camille, sashayed out. Stifling an eye roll, Camille focused her attention on the managing partner. Benson had picked up a baseball encased in a protective plastic shell and was studying it under an official Nats desk lamp. She watched him turn the ball from side to side, reading the signatures scratched into the surface, and wondered what this was about. The man had not come back down here to look at old baseballs.

"I'd like you to sit in on a meeting." For the first time, Camille noticed he had a folder tucked under his arm.

"Okay."

"I would have mentioned it earlier, but I just got the file myself."

"That's all right." Trying not to eye the folder, Camille put on her professional visage. A meeting could mean anything—a gathering of associates, office staff debating the best coffeemaker or even something regarding a client. She waited for Benson to elaborate.

"There's been an intellectual property suit filed against Gowear."

"Really?" Camille recognized the name of Mia's largest client. The outdoor outfitting company had made its name with manufacturing of environmentally friendly clothing and gear. Gowear retained Walker and Jenkins to address a myriad of corporate legal issues. It would be normal for Camille to be brought in on an employment case, but IP was not her area of expertise. "I hadn't heard."

Benson replaced the ball on its pedestal and turned to face her. "It hasn't hit the press yet."

"Who's making the claim?"

"Lulu Fabray."

"The fashion icon from the sixties?"

Benson nodded. "Gowear altered a protected image of her and used it on a promotional T-shirt. Her people want licensing fees plus damages."

"Sounds pretty cut-and-dried."

"Yeah but Gowear wants to keep it out of the press."

"That will be interesting."

"I'm glad you think so." Benson held out the folder. "Welcome to the team."

CHAPTER THREE

Miasma

Camille felt like she was in a bad dream. Seated in the first-floor conference room, she watched a near clone of her younger self detail Lulu Fabray's suit against Gowear. The clone's name was Lillian. An associate attorney, she was Mia's new protégée, and a dead ringer for Camille at twenty-five. It felt like Camille was in a time-travel movie where the heroine crosses paths with herself in another dimension and has to be extra careful not to fuck up the space-time continuum. This was certainly the tea Jenna had wanted to spill. After the meeting, Camille would track her down and make her dump the whole pot.

"Mia thinks Stacey Tabor jumped the gun."

Camille watched Lillian's lips move, but the words didn't register. A thought had occurred to her that was making her feel slightly ill. The woman, this extremely young woman, was almost certainly Mia's lover. Her resemblance to Camille could not be a coincidence. The biggest clue was the clothing. Not only did Lillian possess Camille's curvy, pre-California figure and bobbed blond hair, but she had her clothes and shoes too. The suit. That suit, her suit. It was like Lillian was wearing a Camille costume.

"Mia says that if Stacey had just waited to get the licensing, Gowear wouldn't be facing this suit at all." Lillian tilted her head, calling Camille's attention to a pair of sizable diamond-stud earrings. Mia had given Camille a similar set to mark their first anniversary. She still wore them sometimes. Never again.

If Lillian was aware of Camille's consternation, she didn't let on. "The issue is that Gowear printed and distributed the T-shirts before they got the rights to the photo."

"Did Gowear request permission to use the image?" Camille tried to catch up. She knew she was only getting half of it. This woman, her clone, was making it impossible to concentrate.

"That's the trouble. Stacey got impatient." Lillian tossed her hair. Eight years ago Camille's had looked identical. Mia had made an appointment for her at a salon in Georgetown. When she'd arrived, the stylist had already been given instructions.

"Who is Stacey?"

"Stacey Tabor." Lillian pursed her lips, clearly wondering if Camille had been listening. "Her husband is Jason Tabor. He owns the company. Stacey okayed the T-shirt production before Gowear filed for the license. Now Lulu's people are suing for damages."

"Who owns the image?"

"Lulu."

Camille studied Lillian's beautifully tailored suit. The expensive cut was conservative but sexy, and the buttons were minor works of art. Mia had sent Camille to a French woman on Connecticut Avenue who smelled like cabbage. It had to be the same tailor. The poor girl was even teetering around on three-inch heels.

When Mia had given Camille her first pair of Manolo Blahniks she wasn't able to walk in them. But Mia had told her they made her legs look pretty, so she'd practiced, night after night, until her toes bled. Camille's mother had hated the shoes.

She hadn't understood why Camille would abuse her body for a beauty ideal. When she'd learned that Mia—a woman who kept her relationship with Camille hidden away like a shameful secret—was behind the wretched things, she'd despised them even more. Camille was ashamed that she'd ever worn them. Before heading west, she'd taken anything higher than an inch heel to a thrift store and would have forgotten them forever if it wasn't for the plantar fasciitis that still flared up from time to time. Watching Lillian try to manage the heels was like viewing an early scene from a biopic of her own life. Camille was compelled to warn her. *Save yourself!* Or at the very least, *Save your feet!*

"We'll need to negotiate a number," Lillian was now explaining. "The original licensing fee was never paid, and now Lulu's people want extra compensation to make a point."

"How much?"

"Not sure. Mia talked to Lulu's agent yesterday. Ms. Fabray is notoriously reclusive but we have a conference call with her tomorrow at one."

Every time Lillian said Mia's name it was like hearing a supplicant praise a high priestess. Camille felt her stomach churn and struggled for something to say. "That's good news."

"Mia has a way of talking people into things."

Like your old lady hair cut? Camille choked back the reply. There was zero chance Lillian and Mia weren't sleeping together. The ardent glow of devotion in Lillian's bright green eyes was unmistakable. Camille wanted to pick up the pitcher of chilled cucumber water on the table, throw it into the girl's dewy young face and yell. Warn her to wake up. Hurtful thoughts bobbed to the surface like dead fish in a poisoned pond. Thank God Mia was out of the office for the day. Meeting Camille 2.0 was a curveball that Camille needed to process without an audience. She'd always thought Mia's fear of commitment was to blame for the failure of their relationship. She'd never considered she was just a type and completely replaceable. Right down to the shoes. Ouch.

Camille worked to hide her dismay while Lillian, oblivious, rambled on about Lulu's claim. From what she'd heard so far, Camille couldn't understand why she was having this meeting. Benson certainly hadn't offered a reason and she hadn't asked. As a senior associate, Camille was billed out at the same rate, no matter for whom she was working. But it was odd. The circumstances of the Gowear case, though interesting, had nothing to do with employment law. Why was Camille being consulted?

"It started as a one-off, but now Gowear wants to keep making the T-shirts because the public adores them."

"What do you think of the design?"

"I like it."

"May I see?" Camille was curious.

"Sure." Lillian handed Camille a black-and-white picture of a woman wearing knee-high, go-go boots. Long glossy hair, short trapeze dress—she was dancing on a pedestal at a London club. Camille couldn't have named the model but the photo was very familiar. It was iconic. So not only had Gowear used it without permission, they had altered it by superimposing their logo to run up one of the woman's boots. A caption beneath the image read, "Go-Go with Gowear."

"I know this picture."

"It's pretty famous." Lillian smiled. "Mia says Lulu Fabray was in a few Elvis movies."

"Really?"

"Mia loves Elvis."

Lillian's eyes shone with such adoration that Camille looked away. Had her own affair with Mia been this obvious? Had Camille been such a sycophant? She added the questions to the growing list of things she planned to ask Jenna.

"Mia thinks the case will settle quickly." Saying her lover's name caused Lillian's eyes to sparkle anew.

Camille couldn't help herself. "Mia's probably right," she offered softly, and was rewarded by an enthusiastic grin. The poor girl had it bad.

"The problem we're facing now," Lillian continued, "is that Gowear doesn't want the dispute to become public. They're very brand conscious."

She pushed a glossy catalog across the table at Camille. On the cover, a rock climber was hanging from a precipice by the tips of her fingers. The camera angle was such that the Gowear logo could be seen on both her T-shirt and shorts. Camille's eyes were drawn to a tattoo of a floating lotus-blossom on the woman's chiseled bicep, then to a strip of taut midriff exposed by the climber's acrobatic position. She knew she'd lingered a bit too long on the woman's body when Lillian politely cleared her throat. Camille flipped through the remainder of the catalog, carefully assessing the images. Finished, she put the catalog down on the table.

"So the brand is young, outdoor, and fit." Camille ticked off the first descriptors that came to mind. "How is that jeopardized by an intellectual property claim? It was just a mistake."

Lillian gestured to the file Benson had given Camille. "When you have a chance to check that out, you'll see the Gowear brand has political involvement beyond the environment. Their CEO and founder is outspoken on many issues. Consequently, their customer base tends not to be too forgiving of…"

"Mowing over the little guy?" Camille finished the sentence for her.

Lillian nodded. "Mia said you were sharp." Her eyes sparkled again, and Camille was reminded of how the Kardashians reacted when Joe gave them catnip. She couldn't resist testing the prod once more.

"What else did Mia tell you about me?"

"Nothing you wouldn't have me repeat, I'm sure."

Camille heard the cool timbre of a familiar voice over her shoulder and knew Jenna's intelligence was untrue. Mia was not, in fact, out of the office. Mia was standing right behind her. Camille watched with fascination as the green sparks in Lillian's eyes ignited into full-blown fireworks. Before Camille could rise to greet her, firm hands pressed down on her shoulders, keeping her in place.

"Don't get up, please. There's no need."

Camille fought the urge to push the hands away. When she'd thought Mia no longer had the power to affect her, she'd been mistaken. Camille wanted to scratch her eyes out. She waited a beat before rising from her chair. She and Mia were now eye-to-eye. The vantage point seemed odd, until Camille remembered that she no longer wore the ridiculous heels. On solid ground, she stared down her former lover. If Mia felt any tension, she didn't betray it. Leaning her body back, she cocked her head to the side in a practiced gesture, coolly assessing Camille. "Hello, Camille."

Camille stared boldly back. Narrowing her eyes, she looked Mia up and down. Though still attractive and noticeably fit at forty-five, the natural light in the conference room wasn't doing her any favors. The faintest line of demarcation where her makeup ended edged her face like a mask. Something in Mia must have sensed the exposure, because she stepped purposefully back, out of the sun like a vampire.

"Good morning," Camille said. She looked directly into the almost-black eyes that gave nothing away.

"Has Lillian brought you up to speed?"

If Mia could stand there and pretend they hadn't fucked each other silly for the better part of two years, Camille could too. "She's briefed me on the case, yes."

"And?"

"To be honest, I'm not sure why I'm here."

"Lillian must not have done an adequate job briefing you."

Camille hazarded a glance at Lillian and was not surprised to find her fighting back tears. Camille knew too well the sting of Mia's subtle, public put-downs. She rose to the young woman's defense.

"Lillian did an excellent job outlining the claim. The case seems pretty basic. I just don't understand why you brought me in. I do employment work now, Mia." Camille flinched as she said the name for the first time. A word breathed so many times in passion. And too many times in pain.

"I'm aware of that. As you said, the casework is fairly routine. I'd like you to supervise Lillian."

Camille blanched. There was absolutely no need for her to be handling this case with Lillian. None. "May I ask why?"

"Because I'm busy with other cases and I want the best outcome for my client and the best instruction for my protégée. This will be an excellent experience for her."

Camille knew this was the closest Mia would ever come to admitting to a relationship with Lillian. Lillian seemed to know it too. Her formerly deflated face was now alight with happiness. The whole spectacle made Camille ill. She felt a strong urge to bolt.

"Is that all?"

"It is."

Camille gathered the Gowear paperwork from the conference room table and slid it into the soft leather bag that served as both her briefcase and purse. Turning her attention from Mia, she addressed Lillian instead. "Do you have a hard copy of the demand letter?"

"No, I…"

"Print one out. Bring it by my office tomorrow at ten and we'll map out a strategy for the phone call."

"Your office?"

"I'm in Nationals Park. It's at the end of the hall. You can't miss it." Ignoring the confused look on Lillian's face, she turned to Mia. "I'll check in with you when we have something."

"Early next week?"

"Will be our goal."

"Fair enough."

Camille didn't begin shaking until she'd left the conference room. Bypassing her borrowed office for fear of venting her frustration on innocent bobbleheads, she left the building entirely. Fingers trembling she punched Cory's number into her cell phone but it went straight to voice mail. What the actual fuck? Had her own fawning devotion to Mia been this obvious? Had people felt sorry for her? Had she been a joke? She'd cast herself in the role of spurned lover, but never victim. Observing Lillian's dynamic with Mia was like looking at the world through a new lens. No wonder she felt vertigo.

Camille sat down on a bench near the front entrance where secretaries often gathered to have lunch. Inset into the backrest was a small brass plaque commemorating the love of Caspar and Sheila. Camille smoothed her thumb over the inscription. She'd never expected her name on a bench, but she had asked more of Mia. The relationship had been over for a long time, but the rejection still stung. Why was Mia approaching her now? Was she testing Camille to see if their dynamic still existed? Was that it? Supervising an associate wasn't out of the ordinary. But why this associate? Why this client? It didn't make sense. The aggressive way Mia had forced this project on her was shocking. It was a blatant swagger-hag power trip. She'd physically held Camille down in her chair. What the actual fuck, indeed? Is that what their entire relationship had been like?

Camille rose from the bench and began walking down New Hampshire Avenue toward Dupont Circle. Exercise would clear her mind. She needed to formulate a plan. Until her partnership was announced, she had no choice but to play nice. Fortunately, the Gowear case was simple. Lulu Fabray would present a number and Camille would do everything in her power to make that number smaller. In the interim, she'd avoid Mia whenever possible. With any luck she'd be back in California within the month with both her job and her pride intact.

Their affair had begun when Camille was twenty-five years old and fresh out of law school. Mia was ten years older and a legal phenom. She was also beautiful and the youngest woman ever to be named partner at Walker and Jenkins. In legal circles, she was famous for getting what she wanted.

The instant her nearly black eyes had locked onto Camille, Mia had wanted her. It had all happened so quickly, Camille didn't even remember their first kiss. Mia had moved in on her like an invasive ivy. Camille had been powerless to stop her and zero interest in doing so. How did one spurn the sexiest, most dynamic woman she'd ever met?

The affair had remained strictly private. Only Camille's parents and a handful of close friends knew they were involved. No-fraternization rules were standard practice at all the big firms, in place to discourage sexual harassment claims. Initially, Camille hadn't minded. Sneaking around had even seemed sexy, sophisticated. Their relationship was no one's business. It was private, theirs and theirs alone.

This rationale had worked until it hadn't. A year in, Camille had begun to feel like an object. Interactions with Mia had become rote, their sex life like a weekly tennis match. They'd work up a sweat—maybe challenge each other, maybe not—and then hit the showers. The hard part was that Camille had felt the potential for a greater connection that had never materialized. It took another year of frustration and a deathbed plea from her mother to drive home the fact that the relationship wasn't going to change because Mia didn't want it to. The woman was getting laid and calling all the shots. What was there to fix?

The last straw was when Mia had failed to attend Mary Robbins's funeral. Though Camille had stood in the church for nearly two hours accepting condolences, her lover had never appeared. Breaking away from her hadn't been easy. Mia had taken steps to block Camille's transfer to San Francisco and only backed off when Camille had threatened to file a complaint with HR. It was ugly. Camille had thought of it as a horrible finale to an otherwise interesting TV show where there wasn't going to be any second season. Now she didn't know what to think.

In an effort to calm herself, she took deep breaths and started walking. She didn't realize where she was going, until she looked up and saw the sign for the Metro. It was only eleven thirty in the morning but home suddenly seemed like a good idea. How very impressive. Her first day in the office, and she'd made it exactly three hours.

There were far fewer people on the escalator than during rush hour, and she passed no one as she began her descent toward the station. She walked more quickly, thinking of how happy her father would be if she surprised him with Lebanese food for lunch. She wondered if the place down the street from the zoo was still open. Its tender kabobs and rich stews had made many a family meal. It was only a few blocks from her house and had the best hummus in town.

"No Salt-N-Pepa, this afternoon?"

Camille was surprised to see the same woman she'd seen that morning, now on the opposite ascending escalator. She too was walking and smiling that same flirty grin.

Camille smiled back. "Baba ganoush and baklava, I'm afraid."

They both stopped walking and turned to check each other out. Camille knew she was being obvious but couldn't drag her eyes away. In the small glimpse she'd had earlier that morning she recalled thinking the redhead was attractive, but the three hundred and sixty-degree view was another experience entirely. The woman was long, taut and sexy as hell. Dressed in tight black athletic gear, she was either coming back from a workout or did something physical for a living. Maybe she was a superhero.

"You're making my mouth water." And she was a total flirt.

Though they'd stopped walking, the escalators had continued to move. Soon they'd be too far away to talk without shouting.

"Too bad it's too early for a drink," Camille said, surprising herself with her boldness but was rewarded when the flirty smile morphed into a one of sweet surprise.

"Raincheck?"

"Sure."

The redhead beamed again. "Have a beautiful day, beautiful."

Camille watched her disappear up the escalator, then resumed skipping down the stairs. A beautiful woman had just called her beautiful. Despite the direction of the escalator, things were looking up.

CHAPTER FOUR

Go Where?

The mother cat jumped onto Camille's lap and looked up searchingly into her eyes. Camille only knew it was the mother because she was the smallest of the family. Kris, as Joe called her, must have mated with a much larger breed of domestic feline, as she was outsized by the resulting Kardashian spawn. This was the first time the diminutive tabby had ventured into Camille's personal space. She wondered to what she owed the pleasure. The cat looked at her intently and began to purr.

"I don't have any drugs, Kris," Camille whispered, hoping not to disturb her father who was dozing on the futon under the cat condo in the adjoining room. Joe Robbins kept the Kardashians happy by giving them endless amounts of catnip. It was a questionable practice, but the Kardashians weren't complaining. They genuinely adored her father who, in turn, spoke to them as if they were his beloved grandchildren.

Camille was seated at the dining room table. In front of her sat the Gowear file, a yellow legal pad, and her laptop. After the infuriating meeting with Mia, she'd begun working mostly from home. Jenna accused her of running scared, but Camille knew it was just the opposite. The thought of Mia made her too angry to concentrate. For two years the older woman had used her, pushing her into a box, bringing her out on a whim to fuck her mind, body, and soul. On some level, Camille had always known this, but meeting Lillian—or Throwback Thursday, as Jenna had taken to calling her—had caused the emotion to hit home. Camille felt used. Though she'd been a willing object, totally and one hundred-percent malleable, Mia had still taken advantage of her. Now, there was a very good chance she was doing it to someone else. Camille was afraid if she saw Mia again, she might punch her.

Cory was desperate for Camille to confront Mia. He was now back in California, but had offered to come to DC and be Camille's wingman. But Camille had declined. Her plan was to avoid Mia and so far, she'd been successful. She only went to the office in the mornings. Mia never arrived until after eleven. By that time, Camille was on her way home with fresh pastries and the *New York Times*. Today, she'd have to go back to the office because she'd left her phone. She could picture it sitting on a shelf in front of the framed photo of Beverly Stanley standing on home plate. Camille planned to retrieve it when the workday was done. She'd go in at six, maybe catch up with Jenna.

"Ciao, Camille."

Martina emerged from the kitchen holding a brimming bowl of pasta Bolognese and a glass of water with a blue bendy straw.

"That smells great."

Martina stopped short, a knowing look on her beautiful face. "Don't worry, there is more for you in the kitchen."

"That makes me so happy."

Kris began to pedal her feet into Camille's stomach.

"She's marking you," Martina observed, continuing on to the TV room.

"What?" Camille blanched. Every time she'd heard of a cat marking something, it usually resulted in that something being thrown in the garbage or burned in a barrel. She was very attached to the button-fly army fatigues she was wearing. She tried brushing the cat off her lap but Kris only settled more firmly into her task, pushing repeatedly into Camille's stomach like she was a ball of dough. Camille called softly after Martina.

"Is she going to pee on me?"

"Pee? No."

"The cat is kneading you," Joe yelled from the futon.

"The cat might need me, but I do not need this cat," Camille joked in return and her father laughed.

Martina positioned the pasta and glass on a table where Joe could reach them. She began fluffing his pillows. "You should be honored, Camille. That is her way of showing affection. This mother cat is very sweet." She eyed Kim and Kourtney who were attacking Rob high up on the cat condo. "But she has no control over her children."

"They're just kids," Joe argued.

"Kids who are crazy from the drugs you give them." Martina walked away from the futon and into the dining room where Camille was still seated with Kris in her lap. "Poor mama. Your babies are addicts."

"Addicts?" Joe protested. "Surely that's a little harsh?"

"I will find them jobs." Martina scratched Kris adoringly under her chin. "There is a cat café in Georgetown. We will put your lazy children to work. Mama can stay home and be spoiled."

"A cat café!" Joe perked up. "I want to go."

"We will all go when you are feeling better," she promised him. "We can pick up job applications for the addicts."

Camille lifted the cat off her lap and handed her to Martina. Looking at the smiling woman, she felt a pang of guilt. She'd told Steve Benson she needed to work from home because her father needed her. The white lie couldn't be further from the truth. Martina was participating more and more in Joe's daily care. Most days she lingered after their PT sessions to make dinner or to play cards. She couldn't seem to stop herself from going beyond the prescribed duties of a physical therapist and Camille wasn't complaining. In the two weeks Martina had been working with Joe, she'd noticed remarkable improvement in him. He seemed happy. Martina even had Joe eating vegetables. They were mostly fried, but they were vegetables.

Each day Martina timed Joe's therapy to allow for a midmorning break. The three of them would work the crossword puzzle while eating the pastries Camille picked up at the bakery outside the Metro. It had become their ritual. Her father had an encyclopedic knowledge of pop culture. Martina covered the classics, international geography, and anything language-related. Camille rounded out the trio with politics and sports.

Martina carried the mother cat over to Joe and placed her on his lap. Kris arched her back into his hand as he lovingly stroked her fur.

"Kris would never let her children work in a café, Martina. She loves them too much. Just like the real Kris. Right, Camille?"

"They could be twins."

Camille's disdain for pop culture was no secret. Joe had ruined it for her early on. Her entire life, she'd been subjected to a running diatribe on how public perception was shaped by vast media conglomerates. Joe believed, and he'd published three books on the subject, that these entities controlled everything from the food she ate to the clothing she wore. *You may think you have personal preferences*, her father would say, *but your opinions are actually being spoon-fed to you by big business.* Middle-school Camille had not appreciated any of this. How dare he explain away her Spice Girl obsession as mere consumerism? What did he know about her crush on foxy Ginger? The way she felt in her soul when she looked at the poster of the beautiful redhead? To thirteen-year-old Camille, it hadn't felt manufactured.

Lately, her mind had been on another redhead. Camille had crossed paths with the hottie-escalator woman five times more since the miracle twofer on the first day of work, but still had no idea who she was. The only clue to her identity was that she always wore high-tech workout gear. Jenna had decided she was either a yoga teacher or an heiress. Three times Camille had only been in a position to wave, but twice more they'd exchanged flirty banter. The lanky redhead was audacious. She made no secret of how much she enjoyed looking at Camille's body. Earlier that morning, she'd complimented Camille's top in a way that made it clear she was not talking about her blouse. The attention was like a salve to Camille's battered ego. It was shameful how much she needed it. She'd even changed her sacred early morning ritual to time her escalator rides to coincide with the eight thirty sweet spot when the woman usually appeared.

The Kardashian sister-cats raced madly into the room, fighting over a catnip mouse. Chasing each other around the coffee table, they caused an instant commotion. Camille knew they were the girls, because Rob rarely left the cat condo. Currently he was sprawled on the highest plateau, basking in a ray of sunshine from the transom above the bay window.

The doorbell rang, surprising them all. In a single fluid movement Kim, Kourtney, and Khloe shot up Joe's futon and onto the cat condo where they knocked Rob from his perch. Yowling, he leapt to the futon and knocked Joe's crutch to the floor.

Martina leaned over to retrieve it before moving to answer the door. Hand on the knob, she turned to Camille. "Are you expecting someone?"

"No." Camille stood up, taking position behind Martina in the entrance hall. "Dad?"

"Yes. I'm waiting for Godot, Guffman, and Superman."

"Oh, I hope it's Superman," Martina said. The bell chimed again, and she opened the door.

"Mind the cats," Joe warned.

Camille was surprised to see Lillian teetering in the entranceway holding a dry cleaning bag. The young woman looked pointedly at the crutch in Martina's hand and then up at Camille. Camille could almost see the wheels in her brain spinning as she realized Camille had lied about being needed at home. Lillian might be foolish in love, but she'd graduated near the top of her class at NYU. Jenna had Googled her.

"I'm sorry to barge in," she said and held up Camille's phone as an explanation. "You left your phone at work."

"Thanks."

Camille stepped forward and took the device. She knew her body radiated displeasure at the home invasion but was powerless to conceal her reaction. Lillian standing on her doorstep felt like a violation. What was the woman doing at her home? Martina glided elegantly out of the room and Camille heard the paneled doors closing discreetly behind her. She struggled to choose the right words.

"It's very thoughtful of you to bring me my phone, but you needn't have come all the way to my house."

"It was no problem, really. I needed to talk to you anyway."

Camille was immediately on alert. Her only association with Lillian was the Fabray settlement, where negotiations had come to an unexpected standstill. After receiving Gowear's very generous settlement offer, Lulu had decamped to an ashram in the Arizona desert to mull it over. Her agent expected to hear something by Earth Day—nearly three weeks away—when Lulu felt the collective consciousness of positivity would provide greater clarity. It was infuriating. The case should be over but they were still in the preliminary stages. But maybe something had changed. Maybe Lillian knew something. It had to be why she was here. "Did something happen with Gowear?"

Lillian bit her lip and shifted her weight on the three-inch heels. "Yes. But it's not about the settlement. Gowear is hosting their annual party tonight. Mia was able to get you an invitation." As always, when mentioning Mia, her voice rose in pitch.

"I don't understand. What party?" Camille took pity on the girl, who looked like any minute she might tumble over like a felled tree. "Would you like to come inside and sit down?"

Lillian seemed hesitant but agreed. "Okay."

She stepped gingerly over the threshold and into the foyer. Camille considered where best to host the impromptu meeting and decided on the kitchen.

"Can I get you some water?"

"Sure." Walking tall, Lillian followed Camille to the kitchen.

"Do you want to hang up your dry cleaning?" Camille indicated a row of hooks by the basement door and then reached into the cabinet for a glass.

"Oh. It's not dry cleaning." Lillian's fingers curled nervously around the sides of the plastic sheath. "Mia sent you a dress."

"What?" The tumbler slipped in Camille's fingers but she managed to regain control before it fell to the floor.

"It's because the Gowear party is tonight. Mia didn't want you to be caught off guard." Lillian tried to hand the garment bag to Camille who waved it off like it was a pamphlet on how to join the NRA.

"Thoughtful, but completely unnecessary. I do have my own clothes."

"Of course you do. As you say, Mia was just being thoughtful." Lillian tottered over to the hooks. Leaving the garment bag dangling on the wall, she took a seat at the kitchen table. Camille blinked hard. Thank God her father couldn't walk in here. One look at Lillian and he'd be talking *Twilight Zone* for hours.

"The party is going to be amazing. Gowear rented out the 9:30 Club. The theme is Cirque du Solange." She shook her head. "I know? Right! Solange Knowles and trapeze artists."

"You're kidding." Despite her disdain for all things Mia, Camille was intrigued. The 9:30 Club was the best music venue in the city. Couple that with Solange Knowles and it was a bona fide event.

"Sorry it's such late notice. But it's the hottest ticket in town and Mia didn't want to mention it until she received confirmation that Gowear could add you to the guest list."

Camille handed Lillian the glass of water and sat down at the table next to her. If her name was officially on the guest list, she'd have a hard time declining the invitation. "But why would she put me on the guest list? I'm only working on one case. Surely, I don't get invited to their prom."

"Their prom?" Lillian laughed. "I love it! It *is* their prom, and it's going to be awesome. I'm so glad you're coming."

Camille looked at Mia's mystery garment. "Yippee."

After a few more minutes of awkward conversation, Camille showed Lillian out. Martina was not far behind. By three p.m., Camille and her father were watching a *Jeopardy* rerun on the television in his office. It was hours before the Gowear event, and Camille welcomed the opportunity to escape into the game show. The host, Alex Trebek, was being especially snarky today. Camille had the distinct impression he did not care for Aaron from Dubuque.

Joe Robbins articulated the most probable reason. "Aaron is a nincompoop."

"Dad," Camille protested. She expected Aaron from Dubuque wasn't stupid, just slow on the draw.

"Who is Theodore Roosevelt?" Joe yelled, snapping his fingers when Trebek confirmed it was the correct answer.

Aaron from Dubuque had answered Franklin and lost six hundred dollars.

"Birk," Joe muttered as the Iowan's score plummeted to negative three thousand dollars.

"Your mother was a huge fan of Eleanor," he continued conversationally, and Camille's attention piqued.

"Really?" Of course, Camille already knew of Mary Robbins's fixation with Eleanor Roosevelt. Wasn't there a whole shelf in the basement devoted to the limited edition Eleanor Toadsevelt figurines her mother had procured from Franklin Mint? But her father almost never referenced her mother. Since Camille had returned home he hadn't mentioned her once. To keep him talking, Camille pretended it was new information.

"What is aubergine?" Joe said to the television, and then turned back to Camille. "Yes, Mrs. Roosevelt was an early civil rights activist. It was your mother's cause too. She loved nothing more than a good rally, your mother. And marching! Your mother loved to march." Joe smiled, reminiscing about his wife, and then seemed to remember who he was talking to. "But you know this. You were with her more often than not."

"I was." Camille thought of the endless hours she'd spent standing next to her mother on the National Mall marching for one of the many social justice causes she'd championed. She'd learned about gun control, birth control and, on several frightening occasions, crowd control.

"She had a real passion for equality. She was thrilled when you told us you were gay." His eyes twinkled merrily. "It gave her a new cause."

"She joined PFLAG the next day." Camille's heart swelled remembering Mary Robbins's instant support.

"And then she marched with them in the Capital Pride Parade."

"She was a loud and proud gay mom."

"Her worst fear was that someone would take advantage of you. That's why that woman in your office, the secret girlfriend, drove her mad."

Camille thought of the dry cleaning bag hanging in the kitchen. "That's a particular specialty of Mia's."

"You're well rid of her," Joe said, fixing his eyes back on the television. "Where is Santa Barbara?" he shouted, and then muttered something when Alex said it was San Diego.

Camille rubbed her eyes. There was no escaping the Gowear prom. Mia had made sure of it by putting her on the guest list. Blowing it off would look bad to the client. At least the party sounded interesting. But she couldn't afford to get distracted. She wasn't sure what game Mia was playing, but she would make it clear she was no longer a willing participant. If her former lover wouldn't listen to her, there was always HR.

CHAPTER FIVE

Prom

Camille passed her driver's license to a tiny Goth chick behind the ticket window at the 9:30 Club. Waiting for her name to be checked on the guest list, she experienced a perverse illogical worry that she'd be turned away. It was the time warp thing again, rooted in her high school memories from when the club had been militant about chopping up fake IDs. If they caught you drinking underage, they'd called the police. Camille had used her cousin Katie's Maryland driver's license and lived in terror of being busted. She had memorized all of Katie's personal information like it was her own. To this day, when someone asked when her birthday was, her first impulse was to blurt out her cousin's. When Goth girl looked up through smudged black eyeliner to deliver the verdict, Camille, though she was well into legal territory, held her breath.

"Cool, California," the girl chirped, and flashed Camille a wistful smile. "I was born in Yorba Linda."

The only thing Camille knew about Yorba Linda was that it was the birthplace of Richard Nixon. She decided not to mention it.

"It's a beautiful state," she offered instead.

Goth girl responded with a sage nod. "It's a state of mind."

She slid Camille's ID back through the window together with a pair of black fingerless gloves and a black zip-up vest. Camille noticed the Gowear logo prominent on both items and decided they must be give-away swag. High-tech and slick, they looked like something Cat Woman might wear. Whatever their function, Camille loved them. They possessed the unbeatable combination of looking completely badass and matching her outfit.

Camille smoothed her hands across the soft leather jeans that hugged her body in all the right places. Worn with a fitted black tank top and a wide leather belt, she could be going anywhere. Even the sophisticated Martina had nodded her approval. When she'd come back that evening to play cards with Joe, she had given Camille a pair of thin, silver hoop earrings, and kissed her on both cheeks for luck. Camille had sent Cory a photo and he'd declared her the bastard child of Chrissie Hynde and David Bowie.

When Camille donned the gloves and vest, Goth girl raised her painted eyebrows. "Those are in case you want to be part of the craziness." She nodded to the big double doors leading inside the club. "It's wild in there. People are flying around and shit."

Camille looked hesitantly toward the entrance. She'd spent the better part of an hour researching Gowear corporate. Their parties were legendary. Events with exotic themes and first-class entertainment, each fabulous occasion vying to outdo the last. The previous Fourth of July, the company had rented the roof deck of the W hotel in downtown DC. Bruno Mars had performed a set with fireworks crashing overhead. How could they possibly top that? According to Lillian, invitations this evening were so coveted that Gowear was selling twenty-five tickets for a thousand dollars apiece and donating the proceeds to the American Civil Liberties Union.

Camille had noted upon arrival that the Gowear community was very fit. It was in keeping with the impression she'd gotten from the catalog. She was slightly thrilled to not feel out of place. She may not be as sculpted as the gorgeous climber on the catalog cover, but she was no slob either. Camille was the fittest she'd ever been. The ever-observant Jenna had been correct. The rigid Pilates routine and healthy Californian lifestyle had paid off. Not only did it appear as if Camille could keep up with this crowd, it looked like she belonged.

She pushed through the double doors into the central room of the club. Everyone was dressed in skintight, black clothing. The effect was very *Matrix*, and Camille congratulated herself for choosing the perfect outfit. She'd left Mia's garment bag hanging unopened in the kitchen. Its very existence was an insult. Jenna insisted that it was a power move, classic Mia behavior. Camille couldn't think of another possibility. What was the woman playing at? Why had she insisted Camille attend the party tonight? With a partnership in the balance, it would be helpful to know the answers.

Camille stepped further into the room. A hot, long-haired guy wearing tuxedo pants and a black silk shirt gave her the once-over, boosting her ego. Not her type, but it was nice to be noticed. She flashed him a smile. He started to move toward her when suddenly another man dropped down from the ceiling in front of them. Camille was so surprised she almost walked into a post. When Lillian had said the theme was Cirque du Solange, Camille had thought it meant the backup dancers would be on wires. She'd no idea it meant flying waiters.

The men clipped their vests together. Signaling a rope-handler on the other side of the room, they were soon sailing toward the second-floor balcony where a landing platform had been set up off the center railing. Though it looked sturdy, Camille had no intention of testing it. They could keep their swag—she would gladly give it back if it meant keeping her feet on the ground.

From her vantage point by the door, Camille could see the flyers were controlled by ropes thrown over pulleys attached to the rafters. On the other end of the rope, the handlers steered the flyers by moving about on the floor. It was an elaborate, improvisational dance of controlled chaos. Goth girl had been spot-on. This was some wild shit.

At half-capacity, the club was comfortably populated. Though Camille had been to the venue many times—Jenna had referenced a memorable Al Green concert just the other day— Camille had never attended a private event here. For nearly forty years, the 9:30 Club had been the premiere rock venue in the city. Gowear must be spending thousands to rent the space. Add Solange Knowles and flying people to the mix, and the number must be over six figures.

Camille surveyed her surroundings. The central concert room had no seating and was flanked by bars on either side. Tiered benches facing the stage lined the balconies above.

Lillian had instructed Camille to meet her and Mia at the upstairs bar at eight p.m. Camille had arrived fifteen minutes early to grab a cocktail. A bolt of liquid courage couldn't hurt. On cue, a flying waiter dropped down in front of her carrying a tray of drinks topped with raspberries. He was wearing a tight-fitting harness with a rope attached to the back.

"You've got your flying gear on. Nice." The man winked and handed Camille a glass. His compact body vibrated with positive energy. Beneath the harness he was dressed in hipster street clothes, his hair gelled back dramatically under a porkpie hat.

Camille took a sip and found it was delicious. Berries and coconut working valiantly with another ingredient she couldn't identify disguised copious amounts of alcohol.

"Are you ready to fly?"

"Excuse me?"

The waiter gestured to her gloves. "The Gowear gear means you've signed up to fly, girl. You better watch out. Someone might snatch you up." He gave his rope a hard yank, sending a signal to his handler, then kicked-off from the ground like Peter Pan. It all looked so easy. He sailed to the outside railing of the second-floor balcony where he hung at ease, smiling above the crowd. Looking down at Camille, he tipped his hat. She raised her drink in salute and then took another sip.

The party was truly remarkable. In addition to the flying waiters, a woman was circling the party, high above in the rafters. Camille couldn't make out her face, but the silhouette of her long, athletic shape was clearly visible against the stage lights hanging above her. She watched as the person on the other end of the woman's rope carefully circumnavigated the room. The other three handlers stepped expertly around him as their flyers ferried drinks and Gowear employees between floors. It was easy to see that all four handlers were completely in tune with each other. A good thing, as Camille knew the liability for something like this would be astronomical.

She crossed the floor and mounted the steps toward the upstairs bar. The meeting with Mia and the Gowear executives was in five minutes. This would be the first time she'd seen Mia since day one at the law firm. Camille wasn't sure what her former lover was up to, but she certainly wasn't playing by any rules Camille recognized. Meeting a client was never a casual affair. If her partnership wasn't on the line, Camille wouldn't have come at all. She downed the rest of her drink and set the glass on the bar at the top of the stairs.

Mia stood at the far end of the bar talking to an attractive older man wearing a flying vest and gloves over a fitted Gowear sport shirt and black track pants. The flying clothes were conspicuously absent on Mia, who was wearing a strapless red cocktail dress and high-heeled metallic sandals. There was no sign of Lillian.

The man was laughing at something Mia was saying. Mia smiled, and then spotting Camille, raised her right eyebrow a fraction of an inch. It was a small tell, but enough to communicate her displeasure that Camille had not worn the item in the garment bag.

"Camille, I'm glad you could make it."

"Thank you, Mia."

Out of deference to the client, Camille refrained from sharing her true feelings about the evening. Instead, she gestured to the flying waitstaff and the main stage where Solange was set to perform. "This is just incredible."

"I'm glad you think so," the man said, "but my wife gets the credit. Stacey is the mastermind behind all this. I could never do what she does. I'm lucky to be invited." He offered Camille his hand. "I'm Jason Tabor."

"Jason is our host, Camille," Mia said, and Camille pretended to look thoughtful.

"Jason Tabor, the name rings a bell. Is it possible we've met?"

They all laughed politely at the lame joke. Though Camille had done a cursory Google search to brush up on his biography, Jason Tabor hardly needed an introduction. Tall and spare with a rangy, cowboy vibe, he'd been the public face of Gowear since starting the company twenty years ago. Now he was a national figure and his brand popular worldwide. Jason Tabor was a man of few words but excellent products. The press loved him, and he'd been featured on the covers of *Forbes*, *GQ* and *Esquire*. Camille wondered why it was necessary for them to meet. Gowear must employ hundreds of attorneys. She was working on one case.

"Camille is handling the Lulu Fabray settlement," Mia informed him.

"Oh?" Concern sparked in the intelligent blue eyes. "Stacey's been very anxious about that." He looked around the crowded upstairs bar. "I know she'd love to meet you, Camille. Hear how it's all progressing."

"I'm happy to talk with Stacey anytime." Camille smiled. The Gowear founder was obviously very fond of his impatient wife. He seemed to be far more worried about her feelings than the very large settlement he'd authorized earlier that week. The attitude was unexpected and heartwarming. Camille wished she had better news but endeavored to put him at ease. "We should have it resolved soon. Ms. Fabray is currently on a retreat, but I don't expect any problems."

Tabor shook his head. "Stacey rushed those T-shirts through as a surprise for my birthday."

"I didn't know." Camille shot Mia a look. There'd been no mention in the file of why Stacey Tabor had ordered the T-shirts prematurely. Lillian had given Camille the impression Stacey's act had been self-serving. Camille had imagined Stacey Tabor to be spoiled and impetuous. She hadn't imagined a surprise birthday party.

"Yeah, she was working a go-go theme." Jason smiled indulgently. "You get it. Gowear. Go-go boots. Go-go music. Stacey even hired a Chuck Brown tribute band. Go-go music is a huge deal around here."

"Camille grew up in Washington, DC," Mia said warmly but it hit Camille like an arctic blast. She snapped her head around. How dare Mia claim any knowledge of her life? How dare she make any claims on Camille at all?

"Hometown girl." Jason held his hand up for a high-five and Camille hit it with a little too much gusto. He didn't comment but noticed her gloves instead. "I see you've got your gear on. Have you flown yet?"

"No, but I'm hoping to," Camille lied.

"You need to go out to the platform if you want to catch a ride down to the stage. Personally, I think it's more fun going up."

Camille thought of the joke Jenna would make here and stifled a smile. "I'll keep that in mind."

Jason nodded at a group walking up the stairs, then turned apologetically back to Mia and Camille. "I'm sorry but I need to cut this short. The Canadians have arrived. Can we talk next week?"

"Certainly, Jason. Go," Mia said, as if it were up to her to grant him permission.

"It was nice meeting you, Camille. Thanks again."

"Nice meeting you, Jason."

Together she and Mia watched the CEO depart. When he was safely out of earshot, Mia turned to Camille. Surrounded by glittery people, flying waitstaff and now it seemed, Canadians, this was the first time they'd been alone since Camille had said her final goodbye nearly eight years before.

"You look incredible."

Camille narrowed her eyes. Mia's go-to trick had always been the private-charm offensive. She'd ignore you for hours, and then lay on the flattery so thick you bent to her will under the sheer weight of the compliments. "What am I doing here?"

"I'm disappointed you didn't wear the outfit. My personal shopper spent hours looking for the perfect dress to show off this impressive new physique." She reached out a hand as if to touch Camille's shoulder.

Camille jerked away. "What am I doing here?" she repeated, her annoyance now plain.

"When someone pays you a compliment, it is customary to say thank you."

"I'm not your protégée anymore."

"Then why did you come tonight?"

"Did I have a choice? Lillian made it seem like this was a command performance." Camille looked around for the young woman. She was more than a little curious to see how Mia would treat Lillian in public. When they were having an affair, Mia had acted as if Camille were nothing more than a work colleague whether anyone had been watching or not.

"I thought tonight might be a nice occasion for us to catch up, alone." The dark eyes were suddenly clear with purpose. Doubling down, Mia shot her hand out and caught Camille's wrist, giving it a firm squeeze.

Camille's reaction was swift and violent. In a move she'd learned in self-defense class, she swatted away the offending touch. Stepping back, she tried to keep her voice steady.

"Please do not touch me."

Mia's eyes flashed with surprise, but she kept her voice light. "It wasn't that long ago you wanted me touch to you. Sometimes you begged me. Surely you remember?"

"I remember crying a lot."

They were now face-to-face. Mia's signature Joy perfume permeated the air around them. Though the ceiling was vaulted high above, Camille felt claustrophobic.

Mia reached for her again, and Camille twisted her body to the side. What would it take for the woman to understand that this was not happening?

"I asked you please not to touch me."

"Just have dinner with me."

"No."

Spinning away, Camille walked onto the temporary platform where several party guests were waiting a turn to fly.

Mia stepped purposefully behind her. She wasn't giving up. "You're behaving like a child. Come talk to me. At least have a drink."

Firmly on the platform, Camille rounded on her. "Speaking of children. Where's Lillian?"

Mia averted her gaze. "She couldn't make it this evening."

"You gave me her ticket, didn't you?"

Mia didn't deny it.

"Classy."

"Come with me downstairs to the bar." It was not a request. "Let's go." She held out her hand.

Camille contemplated escape options. When she'd put on the vest and gloves, it'd been purely about fashion. She'd had no intention of flying. Now, it seemed like the only choice.

The platform bounced as a flyer landed behind her. Camille heard a sweet, feminine call over her shoulder. "You ready to get out of here, beautiful?" It was an answer to a prayer.

Camille turned toward the sound. "You have no idea," she began, and then her mouth dropped open. Standing in front of her, the familiar flirty look on her face, was the sexy redhead from the Metro escalator.

CHAPTER SIX

Flying

"Hi." Camille was incredulous.

"So, you ready to go?" The tall woman acted as if running into Camille on a temporary platform, hanging off the side of the upstairs balcony of the 9:30 Club was an everyday occurrence.

"Camille, I want to talk to you." Behind her, Mia's voice was clipped and tight. Camille knew her face must have registered a negative reaction because the redhead giggled. The sound was oddly transporting. The very opposite of the leaden weight behind her.

"I'm thinking, the answer is yes," Camille answered, and the woman's golden eyes danced with mischief. Without waiting for permission, she stepped forward and clipped her vest to the front of Camille's. They were so close Camille could feel the heat of her body.

"Camille," Mia said her name again.

The redhead stepped even closer and Camille detected the faint musk of exertion. It was decidedly intimate, but not the least bit unpleasant. She inhaled deeply.

"Put your arms around my neck."

Camille did as she was told. She'd watched the other party guests fly and knew it was part of the drill. The tips of her fingers brushed against loose strands of red hair spilling from a haphazard bun on top of the woman's head.

"When we lift off, you're going to hold on tighter and wrap your legs around me."

"Okay." Camille swallowed hard. Wrapping her legs around the beautiful body would not be a problem. Knowing Mia was watching from a few feet away would only make the experience more pleasurable.

"Normally, I'd buy you dinner first."

They both smiled at the joke.

Another flyer took off from the platform, party guest in tow like a koala on a eucalyptus tree. The crowd cheered below. Camille watched as the duo spun twice around the room before landing on a mat in the center of the stage.

"We're going to do exactly the same thing. Okay?" the woman said. Camille looked into the golden eyes and was compelled to trust her.

"Okay."

"Camille, please come back here." Mia was not giving up, but Camille didn't care. With her arms wrapped around the neck of the beautiful woman, she felt oddly safe.

"I'm guessing your name is Camille."

"You're prescient."

"No, I'm Hannah." She smiled and her aura was alight with infectious energy. "Ready to go?"

"Camille." Mia tried one last time.

"Definitely."

Hannah turned Camille around to the edge of the platform. An attendant positioned the ropes above them and signaled the handler on the ground. As they prepared to leap, Camille tightened her grip around Hannah's neck. Despite the vests, she could feel the heavy swell of Hannah's breasts against her own. The crooked smile told her the sensation had not gone unnoticed.

"What's your stalker's name?" Hannah asked before lifting off.

"Mia."

"No way."

"Why?"

"It's just too perfect."

"How so?"

"See ya, Mia!" she shouted, and gleefully leapt from the balcony. Camille watched the handler on the ground act as ballast as they were lifted up and above the cheering crowd. Circling once, she looked down and saw Mia's eyes flash with impatience. It was a look Camille remembered too well. With Mia, the argument was never lost, only postponed for another day.

"Don't give her the satisfaction."

Warm breath tickled Camille's neck and she lifted her head to see Hannah smiling at her. Their faces were so close that Camille could see Hannah had a small diagonal scar through her right eyebrow.

"There are much more interesting things to look at. Don't you think?" She looked briefly at Camille's lips, and then back into her eyes. The woman was an audacious flirt. Camille wondered if she might actually try to kiss her.

They spun around the room once more, before slowly making their descent toward the stage. Nearing the landing pad, Camille braced herself for impact.

"I've got you, beautiful," she said, her voice gentle in her ear.

Camille relaxed her grip as they touched down on the mat. Automatically her legs dropped to the ground, and an attendant moved in to unsnap their vests. Camille started to unwind her hands from Hannah's neck when she spied Mia waiting next to the stage.

"Shit."

Hannah followed her line of vision. "We're going back up, Jake."

The man didn't flinch. Re-snapping their vests, he signaled to Hannah's handler positioned at the other end of the room. As Hannah prepared to leap from the stage, he backed away from the pad.

"And, go!"

The handler yanked the rope and once more they were aloft. The ascent to the platform was quick. Hannah didn't take the scenic route this time but propelled them straight forward toward the balcony. Back on solid ground, she unsnapped their vests, and shrugged easily out of the harness that connected her to the rope. Taking Camille's hand, she stepped off the landing pad and began pulling her through the crowd.

Her movements were fluid and efficient, giving Camille the impression that this wasn't the first time Hannah had extricated herself from an unpleasant situation.

"Where are we going?"

"Staff exit."

They made their way behind the tiered seating toward a heavy door at the back of the room. Everyone in the crowd seemed to know Hannah. Many people called her by name. Two gorgeous women wouldn't let her pass without a selfie. As they neared the door, a woman with flat-ironed blond hair and wearing a tiger-print Gowear fleece jacket called for Hannah to stop. But Hannah ignored her.

Squeezing Camille's hand more tightly, she hastened their pace. They approached a heavily pierced bouncer manning the door to the staff entrance. Camille noticed a prominent tattoo of Elmo from *Sesame Street* on his neck. When he opened his mouth to greet them, she knew why.

"How you doing, Hannah?" he squeaked, his large face breaking into a cherubic grin. "I saw you flying out there. When you gonna take me up?" He moved his large body to the side, allowing Hannah and Camille access to the door. Hannah slapped his shoulder as they passed through the entrance.

"Come out to the gym, Rocco, we'll set you up." Hannah was at least five foot ten, but Rocco towered over her like she was a small child.

"Imma bring my girl too."

"You'd better."

The heavy door closed behind them and, suddenly, they were alone in a small room. Directly in front of them was a staircase leading down to a door with a neon sign marked Exit. To the right, Camille saw the VIP balcony that hung over the stage.

Hannah stopped short.

In the dim light, Camille could see open appreciation in her eyes, and her voice was warm and sweet. "Do you want to get out of here? Maybe away from…"

"See ya, Mia?"

They both laughed, and Hannah's throaty giggle echoed pleasantly in the tiny room. She had yet to let go of Camille's hand. Suddenly, kissing her seemed like the most natural thing in the world. Hannah had literally just swung through the air to rescue her from villainous intent. Certainly a kiss was deserved?

The moment was interrupted when two men who Camille recognized as flyers banged into the room. They were drenched in sweat.

"Dude!" the smaller of the two addressed Hannah. "You ghosting?" His tone was inquisitive, not angry.

"Camille and I were just exploring what our options might be." Hannah gently stroked her thumb over the back of Camille's hand. Goose bumps rolled up her arm like waves on the beach. The woman was so sexy. Camille was beyond tempted to see where the evening might take them.

"Won't you get into trouble?" Camille kept her voice low. Hannah was obviously working the party. How would it be okay for her to leave in the middle of the gig?

"It's my company."

"Oh." *Unless she owned the event entertainment company.* Camille hadn't thought it possible, but the hot redhead just got hotter. "Do you have a car?"

"I have a bike."

Hannah stuck a hard K at the end of the word, letting Camille know she wasn't talking about a Schwinn. A hot woman flying through the air was hard enough to resist, a hot woman with a motorcycle was impossible.

"Let's go."

"Later, boys." Hannah saluted the flyers and tugged Camille gently toward the stairs.

"Have fun, ladies," the second man said. Camille thought she heard a knowing note in his voice. He'd probably witnessed this same scenario a million times. Hannah was so warm and sexy, she probably had a new woman every weekend. Camille found that she didn't care.

Hannah pushed open the back door and they stepped out into the alley behind the club. A gleaming tour bus sat idling to the left of a black van. Next to the van stood a shiny purple motorcycle. So far, everything about Hannah had been full-on shero. Of course her motorcycle was purple.

"Is that a Harley Davidson?"

"Yes ma'am, a '94 Dyna Low Rider. It was my mom's. Lemme grab the helmets." Approaching the van, Hannah let go of Camille's hand by degrees, caressing a fingertip in the final contact. The move was practiced, perfect. Camille wondered what those strong hands might feel like on the rest of her body. The evening was definitely moving in that direction.

"Your mom drove a Harley? That's so cool."

"My mom was the coolest," Hannah said but didn't elaborate. She slid the van key from her boot and Camille noticed a floating lotus tattoo on her right bicep. The shape was oddly familiar and Camille did a double take. She'd been transfixed by the Gowear cover model since Throwback Thursday had slid the catalog across the table in the conference room. It was now her screen saver for God's sake.

"You're on the catalog," she stammered. No wonder everyone at the party knew Hannah. She wasn't just an event contractor; she was the Gowear cover girl.

The briefest look of annoyance crossed Hannah's pretty face. Camille couldn't make sense of it. Covergirl seemed in perfect keeping with the other résumé items Hannah had established so far.

"That was not my idea," she replied cryptically.

"Your hair is so much longer now," Camille stammered, still grappling with the coincidence that her screen saver and evening savior were the same person.

Hannah touched the loose bun on top of her head. "Yeah, they shot that ad last summer in the Dolomites. It was hot so I chopped it off."

She unlocked the back of the van and removed two helmets and matching leather jackets. Camille smiled to herself. Of course there were two. Hannah might be a player, but she was not playing around. She handed Camille the gear and, mounting the bike, pulled on her own. "Do you want to take a ride around the monuments?"

"I'd love that." Viewing DC's monuments by moonlight was possibly the most romantic move in the nation's capital. Beautiful marble statuary backlit against the night sky was perfect for a seduction. Camille knew this firsthand. On prom night, her girlfriend Ava had rented a limo and they'd made furtive love in the backseat driving down Independence Avenue. It remained one of the sweetest memories of her life.

Camille wrapped a leg over the Harley and sat down behind Hannah. The passenger seat, though connected to the driver's, sat up three inches higher on the bike. Hannah reached a hand back and ran her strong fingers down the leg of Camille's jeans, flooding her core with warmth.

"I dig the pants."

"Thank you," Camille said and pulled on her helmet. Snapping it into place, she wrapped her arms tightly around Hannah. The small motion pushed her crotch forward against

Hannah's lower back, causing her clit to jump to attention. Her lace thong provided precious little buffer between her pussy and the hard zipper of the pants. The contact would only intensify once Hannah started the engine. If Camille didn't change position, she'd likely come undone in the first half mile.

"You ready?"

Camille moved her pelvis down. She experienced another jolt of arousal at the last brush of contact but managed to hold herself in check. There was no reason to rush things. It wouldn't be long until Hannah made a move of her own.

"Yes."

"Put your feet on the pegs."

Camille did as directed and Hannah started the bike. As the engine roared to life, Hannah released the kickstand, and eased the Harley into motion. Camille held on more tightly as Hannah let out the throttle. She increased the speed slowly until they were cruising smoothly along the asphalt toward 9th Street. The Harley's engine, positioned directly beneath them, created a pleasant vibration that had Camille's own motor revving. She blew out a breath. Harley Davidsons were known chick magnets. She'd also heard them called crotch rockets. Now she knew why.

Bumping onto the main road, Camille shifted positions and, once again, found her clit pressed into Hannah's back. She gasped at the sensation, but her hips pushed forward, following the friction. The pleasure was so intense that Camille couldn't pull away. When Hannah stopped at a red light, Camille was panting for breath.

"Having fun back there?" Hannah called sweetly over her shoulder. Camille's cheeks flamed. When Hannah revved the motor, Camille managed to shift her position, giving her throbbing clit a rest.

Buildings passed by in a blur as Hannah gunned the Harley forward. Camille kept her arms locked tightly around her, snuggling into her back. Her nipples stood at attention, pushing into the leather of Hannah's jacket. If there was more effective foreplay than a zip-line rescue, followed by a moonlight motorcycle ride, Camille wasn't aware of it.

Hannah turned left and Camille watched as Union Station's beautiful façade came into view. Spotlights bounced off the marble and Camille was filled with the familiar sense of hometown pride. A right turn and they were in front of the Supreme Court, the US Capitol building looming over them on the right. Hannah steered the Harley onto Independence Avenue and the streetlights of the stately thoroughfare washed over them like muted sunlight. To the left, they passed government buildings. On the right were the museums on the National Mall. Camille ticked off the names of the buildings in her head as if they were old friends. She knew their order like a kid from Milwaukee might know the lineup of stores in a shopping mall. She also knew which ones had the best restaurants, coolest gift shops, and most accessible bathrooms.

When Hannah turned the bike south on 15th Street, Camille knew they were headed toward the river. She wondered if Hannah would pause by the water or complete the loop and suggest something more discreet. Though Camille was enjoying the ride, the full seduction wasn't necessary. She'd been ready to fuck Hannah since she'd seen the floating lotus tattoo. The Harley slowed and Camille had her answer.

They rolled to a stop along the banks of the Potomac. Hannah killed the engine and dropped the kickstand. Released from her helmet, Hannah's red hair spilled topsy-turvy across her shoulders. Camille carefully removed her helmet and held it between them on the bike. Gently Hannah took it from her hands and hung both helmets on the steering wheel.

When she looked back at Camille, her gaze was full of heat. She licked her lips and let her eyes drop to Camille's mouth.

"Is it okay if I kiss you?" she asked sweetly. "I'd really like to kiss you."

"Yes, please," Camille replied. She grabbed the lapels of Hannah's jacket, and pulled her down firmly against her lips. The moonlight ride had her so turned on, she was having trouble thinking straight. A kiss was certainly okay, but possibly not enough. Camille wanted to devour this woman. Opening her mouth, she greedily sucked in Hannah's tongue, stroking it softly with her own. Passion sparked instantaneously, and when they finally pulled away they were both panting for air.

"Damn."

"Right?" Camille whispered before claiming Hannah's lips again. Kissing her felt like drinking a glass of cool water after a long run. She fought the urge to move too quickly, but Hannah had no such reservations. Removing her lips from Camille's, she slid them down to her breasts, and began nuzzling them through the fabric of her bra and tank top. Camille arched forward, moaning as the soft lips brushed her nipples. The sensation was exquisite. She ached for Hannah to take it further.

"God, Hannah," she moaned again, then closed her eyes. The moment was blissful, heading toward ecstasy. She registered the sound of a car pulling up behind them, but didn't react. This was the perfect spot for a rendezvous. Certainly, they could share. A police siren shattered the thought. What the hell was going on? The siren blared again and Hannah lifted her mouth from Camille's chest, swearing.

"Uh-oh."

Camille opened her eyes to see strobing lights. Reflecting brightly against the water, they lit up the Potomac like a crime scene. A twat-blocking US Park policewoman shamelessly flirted with Hannah for nearly twenty minutes, before issuing them a citation for loitering after dark.

Mood effectively killed, they headed to a greasy spoon in the theater district and settled into a booth.

"So you're from DC?" Hannah fell sideways across the seat. "I was trying to impress you with the moonlight drive on the National Mall. I thought I was being so smooth! You grew up here?" She slapped the vinyl with the palm of her hand, giggling at herself.

"It was a monumental seduction."

"Oh my God, that's so funny." Hannah righted herself in the bench. She ran a hand through her beautiful hair, tucking it behind her ears. Camille couldn't imagine the photographer had been pleased when she'd spontaneously cut it before the shoot in the Dolomites. Hannah probably hadn't even considered the glamor angle. *Now that was hot.*

Watching her now, Camille couldn't take her eyes away. Hannah was a true natural beauty. She either wore no makeup at all or had sweated it all off at the party. The party where she'd rescued Camille by jumping off a platform.

"I can't believe I tried the monument move on a local."

"Well, it's a known winner," Camille said.

"And tonight?"

"Totally working."

"I'm so glad." Hannah beamed.

The server approached and asked for their order. Camille requested tea and toast, the most she could manage after the exotic drink, high-flying escape, and sexy motorcycle ride. Hannah ordered a T-bone steak, scrambled eggs, and pancakes.

"That's a lot of food." Camille was impressed. Hannah's body, perfectly displayed in the fitted catsuit, didn't carry an ounce of extra weight.

Hannah shrugged. "I eat when I'm hungry." She flexed her shoulders causing the stretchy black fabric to grow taut across her breasts and collarbone.

Camille swallowed hard. "You did that on purpose."

"Did what?" Hannah flexed her shoulders again. A low giggle escaped her throat, as she watched Camille bite her lip. "Oh, that?"

"Stop it." Camille shot her a pleading look. She'd barely recovered from the make out session by the river. If Hannah didn't stop teasing her she might combust right there at the table. Hannah seemed to understand and obediently relaxed her body.

"I'm sorry. I'm just really attracted to you." She settled back into the booth, considering Camille. "Where'd you come from?"

"Woodley Park."

"And the woman who was chasing you, see-ya Mia. Is she your ex?"

"Yes, and a hard lesson."

"I've never had one of those."

"A bad break-up? You're very lucky."

"I've never had an ex-girlfriend."

"No way."

Camille didn't try to hide her surprise. Hannah had to be in her mid-thirties. "I find that difficult to believe." She let her eyes wander dramatically across Hannah's body and face. "You've really never had a girlfriend? But you're gorgeous."

Hannah blushed. "Okay, sure. I mean, I've had lots of girlfriends." She made quotation marks with her fingers. "Just no one serious enough to call my ex."

Camille didn't know why Hannah was telling her this. But for some reason, she felt flattered, and found she wanted to continue the conversation. "I've had a few," she admitted, thinking of high school and college. "But it's been a while. Mia was the last serious one, and that was eight years ago."

"Eight years is a long time." Hannah's eyes were warm.

"Yes. I'd like to meet someone, but work gets in the way."

Hannah smiled sweetly at her from across the table. "If only you could meet someone."

Camille smiled back. "If only."

CHAPTER SEVEN

Cat Boxing

Camille pushed open the basement door and stifled a gag. She shouldn't have let it go this long. Her father had warned her. Three days was the absolute max. Four was a new level of hell. Camille pulled the collar of her vintage T-shirt over her face to block out the stench. It only helped a fraction. There was no odor quite like cat pee. She cursed herself for procrastinating and hesitantly approached the boxes.

The situation was entirely her fault. All week long, she'd put off the chore. While cat poo had piled up like catalogs at Christmas, she'd made up excuses. She was too tired from the workday. She would definitely get to it tomorrow. Three days couldn't really be the limit. But it was.

Now she was paying the price. Jesus, Mary, Pop-Tart! What did cats eat that made their urine smell so bad? Thankfully the addiction episode of *Keeping Up with the Kat-dashians* was over. Martina had been very direct. It was either her or the nip.

Camille removed the litter scooper from a bucket next to the boxes and arranged a garbage bag to sit open on the floor. Holding her breath, she opened the lid of the first box.

The catnip situation had come to a head the weekend before. Camille and Hannah had walked into the Woodley Park home the night of the Gowear prom to find Kardashians gone wild. First they'd seen the blood. Then they heard the yelling in rapid-fire Italian. Kim and Khloe had Kourtney cornered in the highest yurt on the cat condo. The sisters were battling for possession of a catnip sock. Joe, as he'd explained later, had fashioned the narcotic footwear in the hopes of weaning them from addiction. Camille suspected that her father, seeking Martina's approval, was trying to distance himself from being the dealer. Whatever the reason, the scene had been catastrophic.

Martina, protecting her hands with oven mitts, was swatting at Kim and Khloe with Joe's Grip-and-Grab reaching stick. Kourtney had the nip sock and was in no mood to share. While the sisters hissed and bobbed like vipers, Joe yelled encouragement from the futon. It was not clear who he wanted to win.

Camille had been struck dumb at the sight, but Hannah had flown into action. Activating a rape whistle app on her phone, she'd sounded a piercing wail, sending stoned cats flying in all directions.

Camille had been so embarrassed, she'd all but pushed Hannah out the door—before asking for her phone number or offering her own. Camille didn't even know Hannah's last name. Stupidly, she'd just assumed she'd see her on the escalator. It had seemed like a given. Camille had taken extra care with her outfit Monday morning, and making her hair look effortlessly perfect. But there'd been no sign of Hannah. The next day it had been the same thing, and the day after. By Friday, Camille had begun to wonder if she'd dreamed it all up. The retelling of the story certainly sounded farfetched. Jenna claimed to not believe a word of it. If there was a superhero lesbian Cat Woman on the loose in the nation's capital, she would know about her. Camille wondered if she would ever see Hannah again.

She scooped the first box and tried not to gag. It was disgusting. It would be far easier if the cats could just go outside. She felt certain they would prefer it. But five Kardashians loose in Woodley Park would almost definitely have a negative impact on the songbird population. Her father would be tarred and feathered with the dead birds.

Camille held her nose and addressed boxes two, three, and four. The bag was getting heavier by the scoopful, but she cheered herself that she was nearly done. A movement caught her eye, and she saw Kourtney coming down the stairs. The big tabby gave Camille a dismissive glance, stepped into the first box, and began to dig.

"Don't mind me," Camille muttered, and then cursed herself for opening her mouth. Choking, she stumbled away from the litter boxes and opened the door to the only other room in the basement. Slamming it shut behind her, she rejoiced in the relief from cat pee—this room smelled like trees, which smelled like childhood.

Flipping on the light, she was hit with a wave of nostalgia. There on custom-built cedar shelves were her mother's frogs. Camille forced herself to step forward. She still missed her mother every day. The collection of frogs was, in essence, a museum of Mary Robbins's life. Each stage had a corresponding amphibious representation. From the cheap tourist-trap frogs collected during her parents pre-Camille days to the rare Murano glass frogs that middle-aged Mary had scoured eBay to find.

Camille smiled through her tears. Hundreds of beady eyes stared back at her. When Camille was a child, Mary had allowed her to play with each and every frog, no matter how precious. From the Royal Doulton porcelain figurine to the Happy Meal Kermit with a chewed ear, Camille had been given free license, *carte verte*.

She'd created lily pad families, acting out their dramas on the green oval placemats borrowed from the dining room so often that they'd eventually found a permanent home in the basement. Camille opened the cabinet next to the couch and found the placemats exactly where she'd left them, waiting for her twelve-year-old self to come down the stairs and spin tales of hop-pily ever after. Her mother had always looked on her games with a fond eye, sometimes even joining in with fanciful stories of her own.

Camille wondered what Mary Robbins would advise her to do about Hannah. Would she tell Camille to cool her jets and wait? The lanky redhead knew where she lived, after all. Or would Mary advise Camille to track Hannah down through the Gowear party planners? Jenna had suggested this numerous times but the idea made Camille feel like a stalker. Though it was getting to the point where she was ready to try anything. Camille tried to hear her mother's voice in her head and sighed as she allowed the long-buried feelings to wash over her.

Mary Robbins's unexpected passing after a brief illness had left a gaping hole in Camille's world. Caught up in her own trajectory, Camille had taken her mother for granted. She'd never once considered the unique role Mary played in her life until she was gone. It was a vacuum of need that couldn't be filled with work or exercise or house renovations. Lord, though she'd tried. Her mother had been her champion. She'd filled Camille with confidence, told her she was smart, beautiful, and special, that she was capable of achieving anything. Sure, these were standard mother attributes, but it didn't matter. Mary Robbins's belief in Camille had inspired Camille's belief in herself. It was the cornerstone of Camille's personal success, the reason she owned her own home and was about to be named partner in a major law firm. What had once been Camille's dreams were now her reality. It was all due to Mary.

Moving along the shelves, a flash of purple caught her eye. She picked up a statue she didn't recognize. Fresh tears began to fall.

"Oh, Mom."

She held the figurine up to the light. About four inches long, it was a shiny, green tree frog sitting astride a purple motorcycle. The fact that Camille had never seen it before was not unusual. She'd stopped playing frog-family in middle school while Mary had kept collecting until her death. Camille blinked hard, and turned the object over in her hand, wondering where Mary had found it. The frog had a sly look on its face that foretold fun. It was solid, pleasing in weight and whimsy. A purple motorcycle of all things. Camille shook her head. Pocketing the figurine, she again cursed herself for not getting Hannah's phone number.

"Talk about a sack of shit," Jenna teased from the window of her Mini Cooper, as Camille exited the basement into the alley behind the Woodley Park house.

"I'd rather not." Camille held the plastic bag containing the cat litter away from her body. She carried it toward the trash can and dropped the bag inside. "I'd rather not talk about it at all." She reached into her purse and rubbed a wipe over her hands and wrists.

"Where are we going, anyway?" Camille asked Jenna, not caring about the answer.

It was a beautiful afternoon. The outside air was fresh and delicious, the glorious day amplified by the heady profusion of flowering plants and trees. San Francisco was beautiful all the time, but DC in true spring was exquisite.

"I'm taking you to Molly's Diner for Ellen Trivia Bingo."

"Sounds fun." Camille ducked into the car and shut the door behind her.

"Holy fuck!" Jenna yelled and grabbed at the door handle.

"What?"

"You stink!" Unsnapping the seat belt, Jenna spilled from the car.

Camille sniffed at her shirt but detected nothing. "I do not."

"You do too," Jenna said from the safety of the alley.

Camille got out of the car and glared at her friend. Jenna was so small, only her eyes were visible above the roof of the Mini.

"Thank God, Melissa insisted we get the convertible." Jenna reached inside the car and lifted a lever that released the canvas top. "Help me fold this back, stinky."

"I used a wipe," Camille protested. She sniffed at her shirt again.

"Use another one," Jenna said and pushed the top down. She moved around to Camille's side, and secured it into place. Walking by Camille on her return to the driver's side, she took a whiff of Camille's hair. "Or ten."

"Jenna!" Camille yelled. "Do I have time for a shower?"

"No." She pushed the door open at Camille. "Brunch starts in thirty minutes. If we don't leave now, we'll lose the table."

Camille got back into the car. She knew better than to mess with a lesbian couple's Sunday brunch, one with a time-sensitive bingo component, no less. She sniffed at her hair but still couldn't detect any odor. Her olfactory nerves may have been obliterated by the stench in the basement. She removed the Purell container from her bag and wiped again at her face and neck.

Jenna nodded her approval and started the engine. Before shifting into gear, she patted Camille's knee. "Don't worry, sweetie. We'll go super fast. Blow the stink right off you."

"Great."

Camille had spent a fractious week with Lillian waiting for Lulu Fabray to sign off on the Gowear settlement. Still in Arizona, the model wasn't showing any signs of moving on the agreement before the promised Earth Day. Camille did not doubt that a collective conscious of positivity would provide Lulu with greater clarity of thought, but Jason Tabor's personal appeal had affected her. He was truly anxious for his wife. Camille wanted to help him, almost as much as she wanted to be rid of Lillian.

When they hadn't heard anything by Saturday, Camille had taken matters into her own hands. Bribing Cory with a fancy spa day in Flagstaff, she'd rented him a car and sent him to the ashram with a copy of the signed agreement and the story of Stacey Tabor's surprise birthday party. If Lulu Fabray possessed an ounce of sentimentality, Cory would find it. Once the settlement was signed, Camille's stint as clone wrangler would be blessedly over.

Lillian had been understandably hurt that Camille had replaced her as Mia's plus one at the Gowear prom. Her edges were still sharp. Several times she'd asked Camille for explicit details of the night. She'd wanted to know how long they'd stayed, and if they'd gone out to dinner after the event. *As if.* Camille had done her best to give plausible answers, while cursing Mia for her callousness. The older woman had been out of the office all week at the partners' retreat in upstate New York where they were making the final partnership decisions. Camille didn't appreciate being left to mind the irate puppy. But with the partnership in the balance, she'd had no choice but to play nicely.

"Are you thinking about the partnership again?" Jenna scolded.

"Sorry," Camille replied and tried to put the case from her mind. Cory had barely been gone twenty-four hours. He'd text when he knew something.

"That's okay," Jenna replied and turned the conversation in another direction, "You know, Melissa's friend Bonnie is really cute."

"You said that yesterday. And you used those exact words. What's wrong with her?" Camille studied her friend. Jenna had many skills. Lying wasn't one of them. The brunette looked pained.

"Nothing!" She turned the car onto Connecticut Avenue and made a big show of focusing on the road.

"Something's up. I can see it in your face," Camille pressed her. "What's wrong with Bonnie?"

"Nothing, *really*. I'm just not sure she's your type."

"Not my type? What are you talking about?" Camille glared at Jenna. She'd only agreed to the blind date because Jenna had given her the hard sell all week. She'd promoted Bonnie as an adorable creature, and now she wasn't Camille's type?

"Melissa thinks you guys will have fun together," Jenna nearly shouted and then rolled her enormous eyes, revealing her sentiments on the issue.

"So this is Melissa's idea?"

"I'm sorry." Jenna looked at Camille like the situation couldn't be helped, like she wasn't aiding and abetting the fix-up brunch by driving across town to pick her up.

"Jenna!"

"Melissa thinks you might click."

"I can't believe this," Camille huffed but didn't continue arguing. There was no point challenging Jenna when Melissa was involved. The woman was completely devoted to her emergency-room-doctor wife. She had been since they'd met on a softball field ten years ago. Their mutual adoration was a beautiful thing. Melissa didn't abuse the power Jenna's devotion gave her but reciprocated in kind. It was what a relationship could—should—be.

"What's the matter with her?"

"I *told* you, nothing. She's cute."

"You said that."

"It's true."

Camille stared at her until it all came out in a rush.

"Okay fine. Bonnie's still obsessed with her ex-girlfriend, all right? Every time we hang out, it's *X-files* on repeat. If we are not extremely careful, brunch conversation will get hijacked." Jenna looked woeful. "But I promise, Molly's scones will more than make up for it."

"Fair enough," Camille replied, enjoying the feeling of her hair being lifted in the breeze. The guarantee of a properly made scone was the best offer she'd had in a while. Well, in a week anyway. She ran her fingers through her hair. The open car reminded her of the night on the motorcycle, the memory of Hannah's lips on hers. She felt for the frog figurine in her pocket and wondered if she'd ever see her again.

CHAPTER EIGHT

Owning It

Jenna steered the Mini Cooper onto 18th Street and they crossed the Duke Ellington Bridge into the neighborhood of Adams Morgan. Despite her malaise, Camille smiled. The diverse, urban community had been a favorite haunt of her youth. The stage of many a caper and milestone. It was less than a mile from Woodley Park, but you could almost imagine you were in another city. They passed ethnic shops and restaurants with bright awnings and colorful window displays. Camille had rented a basement apartment here after law school. The street had been filled with families and young, struggling professionals like herself. It was the first time she'd lived alone, but she'd never once felt lonely. There had been block parties and seasonal holiday decorations. It had been a real community.

Back in San Francisco, Camille was living in a basement apartment again, only this time she owned the house above it. As the timetable on the upper-floor renovations was a moving target, living in the basement made sense. Renting another apartment was ludicrous when the space was perfectly habitable. Yes, it was a big step down from the condo she'd rented in the Presidio with views of the Golden Gate Bridge, but she was really only there on the weekends, when she mostly slept and did laundry. Living onsite had the added benefit of allowing her to speak with the contractors on a daily basis. Camille had found that, much like woodland-fairies, they were only visible in the morning.

Jenna parallel parked into a tiny spot behind a florist's delivery van. She took the keys from the ignition, and tucked them into the pocket of her faded, denim jacket. Leaning close to Camille, she inhaled deeply and then made a face. "Purella Deville!"

"Jenna!"

"I'm just kidding, you smell fine." She pulled a small atomizer of Bleu de Chanel from her purse. "May I?"

"You might as well."

"Great," Jenna spritzed Camille twice and then inhaled again. She nodded her head. "Now you're delicious."

"Oh goodie."

"You know what's also delicious?" Jenna exited the car.

"Scones?"

"Yes! I'm *really* glad you like scones, because that's an important thing."

Camille shut the car door and stepped onto the sidewalk.

"Dare I ask why?"

Jenna gave her a sidelong glance. "Because Kathy is allergic to eggs."

Camille searched her brain for clues but came up with nothing. "Who is Kathy?"

"Bonnie's ex."

"Oh, right."

The two women walked down the sidewalk. Molly's Diner was only four blocks away, but the crush of pedestrians enjoying the beautiful spring day made it difficult to move quickly. The neighborhood was alive with energy. Molly's Diner was not the only brunch option. There were lines out the door of four other establishments they passed. Camille's father liked to say that Adams Morgan was like a woman's wardrobe. It was mostly full of bright, trendy things that only lasted a season or two, but there were also a few timeless gems. Molly's Diner was such a spot. Jenna had been lucky to find a parking place within a mile of the place.

Sunday brunch at the storied, gay-owned diner was *de rigueur* for lesbians over thirty. Today was special. One lucky woman would win an all-expense paid trip to see a live taping of Ellen DeGeneres' popular talk show in Los Angeles. The proceeds benefited the Washington DC chapter of Planned Parenthood. Molly's would be packed.

"So don't order eggs okay?" Jenna repeated.

"Because of Kathy?"

"Egg-xactly."

"I'm confused. I thought it was just the four of us today."

"It is. But mentioning eggs is one of Bonnie's triggers."

"Bonnie has triggers?"

"She does."

"Like a gun?"

"Yes." Jenna stopped short on the sidewalk, and Camille nearly ran into the back of her.

"Jenna!"

"I'm sorry, but this is important." She looked at Camille imploringly, her enormous eyes even wider than normal. "Kathy is from the French Quarter, so don't mention New Orleans either. Actually don't mention Louisiana, or the south at all. Or food."

"I can't mention food?"

Jenna shook her head, and dark curls danced around her shoulders adorably. "Kathy works for a restaurant group."

"But we're eating at a restaurant. How can I not mention food?"

"You can order," she said as if the caveat were obvious. "Just don't ask any questions about the menu." She resumed walking and Camille followed behind her.

"Why?"

"Kathy designs menus."

"Maybe it's better if you tell me what I am allowed to say."

"Yes, probably."

They walked another block, but Jenna said nothing.

"Well?" Camille finally demanded.

"I'm thinking!" Jenna stopped again and pressed the heel of her hand into her forehead for dramatic affect. "You know what? Don't worry about it. Order eggs étouffée if you want. Bonnie will talk about Kathy no matter what we say. There's no stopping her."

Jenna looked so earnest, Camille laughed. She laid an arm around her friend's shoulder as Jenna's phone buzzed with an incoming text.

"Oh God. They've already been seated and are drinking Bellinis. Come on." She quickened her pace, and Camille followed behind, weaving through the crowd. People standing in line outside gave them the side eye as they passed, but Jenna moved too fast for anyone to engage them as she maneuvered them inside the crowded diner.

Scanning the room, Camille recognized Melissa at a table by the window and gave her a happy wave. It'd been at least five years since she'd last seen Jenna's wife, but she'd know the beautiful Nigerian doctor anywhere. The perfect posture was a dead giveaway. Melissa had danced three years with a national company before a torn tendon sidelined her to a life of medicine.

Seated next to her was a petite blond woman who Camille knew must be Bonnie. She was undeniably cute. Jenna had used the descriptor at least three times and, Camille had to admit, her friend had not been exaggerating. Bonnie was *bonny*. She looked like a casting agent's idea of a spitfire cheerleader. Reese Witherspoon would play her in the movie.

They threaded their way through the crowded room toward the table. With the bingo hour drawing near, Molly's was at capacity with urban lesbians of every stripe. On the counter, a life-sized cutout of Ellen DeGeneres smiled sweetly down at the crowd. Even in cardboard form, the celebrity radiated good vibes. Next to cardboard Ellen was a dry erase board, waiting for the trivia answers to be recorded. The atmosphere was festive, and Camille felt a rush of gratitude to Jenna for including her in the brunch. After the lackluster week, it would be a nice distraction.

Melissa stood to enclose Camille in a warm hug. They embraced for a long moment and, letting go, smiled happily into each other's eyes. Camille and Melissa had bonded early, when they'd discovered they were the only wine drinkers among a group of beer lovers. They'd split bottles of pinot noir at dinner parties and prosecco on the beach. Melissa, ever thoughtful, usually brought the wine. Camille's mother had loved her because Melissa met two very important criteria. She always did the dishes when she came for dinner and she looked you directly in the eye when she spoke.

Melissa released Camille and hugged Jenna close. The couple was perfectly matched—Melissa the steady counterpart to Jenna's boundless enthusiasm. Melissa whispered something into her wife's ear and Camille looked away to give them privacy. A plate of freshly baked scones on an adjacent table caught her eye.

"Those look amazing."

"We ordered some for the table. Hi, I'm Bonnie," the woman stood and offered her hand.

"Camille." She waited for a tingle of recognition but felt nothing. Just warm, firm fingers with clean, practical nails.

They all took their seats. In addition to scones, Molly's was also famous for their bottomless Bellinis. A half-finished pitcher sat next to four empty glasses. Two had telltale, first-round residue on the bottom. Jenna picked up the pitcher and filled all the glasses equally.

"I think we're playing catch up, Camille," she said and clinked glasses with her wife, who neither confirmed nor denied the observation. Jenna gestured to Bonnie.

"Bonnie's an ER doctor at Fairfax Hospital with Melissa."

"Oh, that's great." Camille smiled at the woman across from her.

"Yes." Melissa picked up the baton. "And Camille works with Jenna at the law firm."

"In the San Francisco office, actually," Camille clarified.

"Camille is about to be named partner," Melissa added, matchmaker's cap now firmly in position.

"It isn't official yet, Melissa. Don't jinx it," Camille teased, and then purposefully changed the subject. She was just beginning to enjoy herself, the last thing she wanted to think about was work.

"I'm out here for a few weeks, helping my dad out."

"How's he doing?" Melissa asked, and her voice took on a professional tone.

"So much better, thanks." Camille smiled as she thought of Joe Robbins playing Jenga with Martina that morning after physiotherapy. Physically he'd made significant strides. It wouldn't be long before Camille could return to California with a clear conscience. "He was really lucky not to have been more badly injured."

"What happened?" Bonnie tipped her pert little face in Camille's direction, and took a liberal sip of her Bellini. Somehow her glass was nearly empty again. She reached for the pitcher and helped herself to another serving. "Did your father have some kind of accident?"

Camille started to answer but Jenna kicked her under the table.

"He..." she looked at her friend for guidance. There was obviously a Kathy trigger somewhere in the story. "Got hurt," she finished lamely, and then glared at Jenna.

Melissa stepped in. "Didn't he get hit by a car, riding his bike to work?"

Jenna let out an audible squeak, but Camille had no choice but to answer. "That's right."

Bonnie looked totally earnest. "My ex, Kathy, was in a cycling accident a few years ago in Italy."

"Oh, no," Camille replied and watched the same sentiment register on Jenna's face. She took a long gulp of her Bellini and pretended to study the bingo card. Camille knew she was trying not to laugh. Shaking shoulders behind the card suggested she was doing a poor job.

Bonnie was oblivious, and clearly just warming up. "Yes, it was really scary." She put her hand on Camille's arm. "I don't speak Italian. Kathy is fluent, of course. She took it at Smith. Lived her senior year abroad, in Florence. I only speak menu. All the Italians speak English, thankfully. So, it was okay."

Melissa was now looking at her bingo card like it was the road map to Shangri La.

Camille struggled for something to say that would not encourage more Kathy chat. "It must have been so frightening."

"It *was*," Bonnie reminisced happily, and Jenna signaled to the waitress for more Bellinis. "But the hospital food was amazing. Everything was completely fresh. Kathy was served a grilled fish with the head still on. It even had the eyeball. In the hospital. Can you believe that? Of course she couldn't eat the beautiful frittatas."

"No?" Camille looked to Melissa for help. The tall doctor seemed to be deliberately ignoring the conversation now. She and Jenna had completely abandoned Camille to the *X-Files*. There was only one way to deal with this level of neglect. Camille leaned in. "Is Kathy not an egg person?"

Jenna stepped hard on her foot, and Camille kicked back at her. Bonnie remained oblivious.

"That's the tragedy. She's loves eggs. And she *really* loves frittatas. But she's mildly allergic. Too much exposure, and she's covered in hives. We always traveled with an Epi-pen."

"Can you get those through security?"

This time, it was Melissa who knocked Camille's foot under the table.

Bonnie's voice dropped in resignation. "You have to declare them. It's a hassle. But what are you going to do?"

"You couldn't risk Kathy's life."

"No."

The arrival of the waitress saved Camille's foot from further battery. "Everyone ready to order?" The waitress placed a fresh pitcher of Bellinis on the table and picked up the empty.

"Fill 'er up," Jenna said, and Melissa nodded enthusiastically. She leaned over and whispered something in her wife's ear. Jenna smiled, and kissed her cheek. They were wholly loveable. Camille, though still annoyed, couldn't help but smile.

The waitress filled their glasses, and then took out her notepad. "Who's ready?" She nodded at Camille.

"Quiche," Camille replied. The egg conversation now cracked, she hoped it was safe to order as she liked.

"Me too," Jenna echoed.

"I'll have the fruit plate," Melissa countered and Camille knew this meant the couple would share.

"Frittata," Bonnie said sadly.

"What time does Bingo start?" Jenna asked.

"A couple of minutes. We're waiting for the emcee."

"Is someone special hosting?" Melissa wanted to know.

"Ooooh, is it someone famous?" Antenna up, Jenna rubbed her hands together with the glee of a child on Christmas morning.

"Some hot chick from the sponsor. Molly said she was on the cover of their spring catalog," the waitress replied, not realizing she'd just dropped a bomb in the middle of the table. Camille felt her body react and she shifted in her seat to look at the board next to the Ellen cutout. Just as her eyes registered the Gowear logo in the bottom corner, her ears picked up the sound of an engine outside the diner. A familiar motorcycle, with Hannah astride, pulled up in front of the building.

Camille reached blindly for Jenna's arm. "That's her!" she said, a bit too loudly, alerting everyone at their table and a few people next to them. They all turned to watch the lanky redhead dismount the Harley.

"Who?" Jenna followed her gaze.

"Hannah," Camille said, her voice now lower.

"Cat Woman?"

"That's Cat Woman?" Melissa chimed in. She'd obviously been briefed on the pertinent details regarding Camille's interaction with the mystery woman. It was to be expected, Jenna shared everything with her wife.

"Yes, that's her."

"The woman you met on the escalator and snogged by the river?" Jenna was in shock.

Lost in Kathy world, Bonnie looked up from her drink.

"It's weird how I keep running into her." Camille pulled the frog figurine out of her pocket and placed it on the table. "Wherever I go lately, she seems to turn up."

"Did she give you that?" Jenna reached for the toy and began to roll it around on the table.

"No, I was thinking about her this morning when I found it in the basement."

Jenna's large eyes got even larger. "No way."

"Yes, and now she's here." Camille took a sip of her Bellini. "Maybe I conjured her up."

"Voodoo priestess," Jenna enthused.

"I've seen stuff like that happen before," Melissa said, and touched Camille's glass with her own. "There's no denying a powerful attraction."

"Kathy believed in reincarnation," Bonnie offered and sipped her Bellini.

They all watched as Hannah removed her helmet and shook free her gorgeous red hair. As usual, a flirty smile played on her lips. She paused to check out a street musician, and her face became thoughtful. Camille's heart swelled at the beautiful expression on her face. Hannah was completely in earnest, her eyes clear as she listened to the music. She dropped a bill in the man's guitar case and moved toward the door of the diner.

"That's Hannah Richards," Bonnie said in surprise.

"Who?" chorused the other three.

"Kathy's instructor. She took climbing classes at her gym in Virginia."

"What type of class? Wasn't Kathy quite adventurous?" Melissa dove right at it, reminding Camille why she loved her.

"It was a rock climbing class. They started in the gym, then took field trips. Kathy really liked it. She was away on weekends a lot, which sucked for me. But her body looked awesome, so that was a plus."

Camille watched Hannah tuck the helmet under her arm. As always, she was kitted out in sleek workout gear that displayed the contoured lines of her long, lithe body. Camille knew she was staring, but couldn't help herself, and she wasn't alone. The cover model had attracted the attention of half the restaurant. Camille willed Hannah to look in her direction. But she'd stopped at a table near the front and was addressing a group of women. Camille only realized Bonnie was still talking when Jenna cleared her throat.

"I'm sorry?" Camille looked at Jenna with confusion. Why was her friend's mouth hanging open like a dead fish?

"Say that again, Bonnie," Jenna directed the small blonde.

"Hannah Richards is not just the owner of Kathy's climbing gym, and a Gowear catalog model. She owns the company."

"What company?"

"Gowear."

Camille blinked. "Hannah Richards owns Gowear?"

"Bingo."

CHAPTER NINE

Bingo!

"She owns the company?" Camille tried to fit the information into the image of Hannah that had begun taking shape the first time she'd seen her on the escalator. It didn't compute. When Hannah had told her that she owned the company, Camille had assumed she'd meant the one that supplied flying waiters.

"Co-owns, sorry. Her dad owns half." Bonnie drained her Bellini and picked up the full pitcher in front of her. "Kathy told me the story. Hannah's father gave her half interest when he got married a few years ago."

"I knew she was on the spring cover," Camille said softly. "But I had no idea she co-owned the company."

Jenna's reaction was more animated. "Cat Woman actually exists?" She looked at Melissa confirming Camille's prior speculations.

"I'll say she does," Melissa winked at Camille. "Nice job, lady."

Camille blushed, and they all watched as Hannah stopped to talk to a hostess who, unlike Jenna, seemed to know exactly who she was. All over the diner, heads were turned in her direction.

Jenna gave a low whistle. "Damn Camille, she's hot. I mean Rita Hayworth, escape-from-Shawshank hot. I can't believe I had no idea such a creature existed." She covered her eyes in lament. "I'm so out of the loop."

Melissa laughed. Leaning over, she hugged her wife. "When were you ever in the loop, baby?"

Jenna slapped her away. "Back in the day! I knew where all the bodies were buried."

"Back in what day? High school? You were twenty-five when we met."

Camille listened to her friends' banter, while keeping a careful eye on Hannah. She watched her greet three women seated at a table near the front counter and place her helmet under an empty chair. Camille wondered if one of the women was Hannah's lover and was surprised to feel a twinge of jealousy. What was that about? There was every chance Hannah had a lover. Two of the women at the table were beautiful, definite possibilities. Narrowing her eyes, Camille tried to get a read on the relationships.

"Those two are a couple. The older woman is the blonde's mom," Bonnie piped up with the unexpected information. Her voice was so upbeat, Camille knew she was either drunk, or that the source of her knowledge involved Kathy.

"Oh, really?" She tried to look casual, but controlling her face was an effort. At the first sight of Hannah, her heart had begun hammering like a lovesick cartoon cat. Jenna the Antenna was eyeing her with concern. Blessedly, she stepped in to help.

"How do you know them, Bonnie?"

"Through Kathy!" Bonnie slurred and flung her arms dramatically in the air. "The dark-haired woman is Bree, Hannah's business partner at the gym. The icy blonde is her girlfriend. I forget her name. I met them with Kathy at a fundraiser last year. Kathy was wearing the same shoes as the blonde."

"Really?" Jenna indulged her. "What kind of shoes?"

"Jimmy Choo. Black patent leather, peep-toe pumps." Bonnie let out a fractured giggle. "I bet you can't say that nine times in a row, really, really fast."

"You're right." Jenna gestured to the older woman at the table. "How do you know she is the blonde's mother?"

"Just look at them." Bonnie gestured and nearly knocked over Melissa's drink. "They have the same coloring, the same bone structure, and they're both carrying expensive handbags."

Melissa laughed. "Is that your professional opinion, doctor?"

Bonnie nodded her head. "Yes, doctor."

"Well, I'm inclined to agree."

"Me too," Jenna said, and pulled her wife in for a kiss.

"You two!" Bonnie slapped at the table, causing them all to jump. "If Kathy were here, she'd say get a room!"

"Oh, Kathy's here all right," Jenna joked, causing Bonnie to stand up, and knock over her chair.

"She is? Where?"

Camille watched with horror as the poor woman stretched to her tiptoes, frantically scanning the room for her lost love.

Melissa was quick to action. Righting Bonnie's chair, she collected her friend in a sisterly side hug. "It's okay, honey, Jenna's only kidding. You know Kathy lives in New York. Let's sit down and have some breakfast." She nodded at their waitress, who miraculously was making her way to their table with a large tray.

"Okay." Bonnie was too drunk to be embarrassed, but Jenna was properly chagrined.

"I'm so sorry," she said sincerely as the waitress began to put the food on the table.

But Bonnie wasn't holding any grudges. She waved away the apology.

"It's not your fault Kathy left me for a podiatrist. The bunion queen of northern Virginia." She drained her glass. "People and their fucking feet. I treat the whole body, you know," she informed Camille.

"That's amazing," Camille replied. Though physically present at the table, her mind was buzzing with the same word that had been escalating in volume since a certain redhead entered the room. *Hannah. Hannah. Hannah.*

She could only see a fraction of Hannah's face in profile but each glimpse of her was like a bright flash of sun stabbing through the clouds. Camille was dazzled. But the knowledge that Hannah was co-owner of Gowear wasn't good news. There were strict conflict-of-interest rules at the firm. Now that Hannah was a client she'd be considered off limits. Beginning an affair with her this close to the partnership announcement would be an idiotic risk. Knowing this, however, did not stop Camille's chest palpitations.

A small, round woman wearing a lavender Molly's Diner T-shirt approached the microphone next to Hannah's table and switched it on. There was a boom and a caustic screech ripped through the room, silencing the crowd. When heads turned to scowl in the direction of the sound, the woman used the equipment malfunction to her advantage. Through the amp, her voice came out clear and strong.

"I lay awake all night worried about how I was going to distract a room full of lesbians from brunch, and who knew? All I had to do was puncture your ear drums." She paused as the crowd laughed appreciatively. "My name is Molly, and we're here to raise money for Planned Parenthood. You all know the great work they do." A cheer went up. "And if you don't, well, welcome to planet Earth. We're glad to count you in our number. There are pamphlets in the back." The crowd laughed again. "This morning, our Mistress of Ceremonies needs no introduction. Hannah Richards from Gowear. As always, she's giving back to the community in a big way."

The crowd applauded as Hannah rose from her chair to stand next to Molly. She smiled and waved, seemingly unconcerned that more than eighty lesbians, half-drunk on Bellinis, were charting her every move.

"Hannah and Gowear are sponsoring Ellen Trivia Bingo today by donating the grand prize." Molly had to wait a beat before continuing. "The winner today will receive two plane tickets to Los Angeles, hotel accommodations, and passes to see a live screening of the *Ellen DeGeneres* show."

The crowd erupted so loudly that Molly gave up. She handed the microphone to Hannah and then moved over to stand next to the spinning cage containing the trivia questions.

Molly said something inaudible and Hannah cracked up into the microphone. The throaty giggle washed over the room like a warm wave.

"Damn, she's so fucking hot," Jenna said under her breath as all around them conversations ceased. Hannah now had everyone's full attention.

"Thanks for the nice welcome, Molly. And thank you for hosting the event in your amazing diner." She gestured to the crowd, who answered with a loud cheer of appreciation for Molly, who executed a surprisingly graceful curtsy. Hannah approached the Ellen cutout, and gave the talk show host a tight salute. "And thank you Ellen."

The brunch crowd cheered again and someone screamed, "We love you, Ellen!"

Hannah beamed.

"I do too," she said sincerely. "Anyone who wins today, feel free to take me as your plus-one."

"I'll take you, Hannah," a very large woman of seventy-plus years said solemnly from the front row, and everyone laughed.

Hannah batted her eyes. "I'll hold you to that, Sue." She pointed to the rolling cage. "Ready to get started?" The crowd cheered. "Everyone have one of these?" Hannah held up an Ellen bingo card. "This is how it works. I'm going to read a piece of Ellen trivia. If the corresponding answer is on your grid, mark it. The first person to get five squares in a row—horizontal, vertical, or diagonal—yell Bingo! Any questions?"

"What are you doing later?" a woman who was sitting behind Camille shouted.

Hannah didn't miss a beat. "Well, I just got back into town. So I need to do some laundry." She stopped short as a sweet smile of surprise formed on her face. She'd seen Camille and was staring at her openly above the crowd. Heads turned to see what she was looking at, but Hannah didn't rush the moment. Unconcerned, she just smiled at Camille, like they were the only two people in the room.

"But now that I think about it, I'm hoping a friend of mine can hang out."

"Cat Woman on the prowl," Jenna squeaked, prompting Melissa to shush her.

Camille was unable to form a coherent thought. But her face responded for her. Answering Hannah's question, her lips tipped up into a radiant smile that flushed her body with heat. The Molly's crowd, who was following the exchange like it was the final point at Wimbledon, cheered accordingly.

"Okay, so my day just got so much better." Hannah pointed to Camille as if she were now part of the show. "You know this is why I was almost late today? I was bringing flowers to this lovely woman's house. I didn't get her phone number the other night and, like I told you, I've been out of town." She turned toward Camille. "I left them with your Dad's girlfriend, she's really nice."

Camille smiled, and did her best to act as if this were completely normal and not like a scene from a Julia Roberts movie. Her mind spun in every direction, stopping mostly on glee. She'd just been publicly claimed by the most eligible lesbian in the city. Yes, the woman was a client. But when Camille looked into Hannah's golden eyes, it didn't seem to matter at all.

Camille could feel the attention of the crowd, especially from the three women at Hannah's table. She took a long sip of her drink as her mind continued to race. Jenna squeezed her fingers under the table, bringing her back to earth. Hannah was finishing her story. "What's the lesson here, ladies?"

"Always get her number!" shouted more than one patron.

"Can I hear that again?"

"Always get her number!" chorused the restaurant.

"Exactly." Hannah spread her hands in a flourish, and then clapped them together. "Fortunately, I get a do-over." She flashed her flirty smile at Camille, and the crowd hooted. "Now who wants to play bingo?"

"We do!" answered the crowd.

Jenna opened her eyes impossibly wide and hissed between her teeth. "I think you have a date."

Camille gave her a tight smile and tried to pay attention to the action at the front of the restaurant. The cage had completed its first spin, and Molly was fishing out a clue. She handed a scrap of paper to Hannah who read the printed question aloud.

"What state is Ellen from?"

Camille looked down at her card. The words were perfectly legible, but she couldn't make sense of the answers. She knew Jenna was in a similar frame of mind, because the smaller woman was now squeezing Camille's wrist under the table like she was hoping to extract juice. Though painful, the sensation was the only thing keeping Camille from floating away. Melissa seemed tickled by Camille's agitated state. Bonnie was playing bingo.

"Ellen is from Louisiana," Bonnie whispered loudly to the table, "But not from Baton Rouge. Kathy is from Baton Rouge."

"Thanks." Melissa marked her card, and then reached over and marked Jenna's. Camille's had fallen to the floor and was pinned under the leg of a chair. Molly spun the cage again and fished out the next clue for Hannah to read. Hannah's eyes danced playfully as she flirted with the crowd but the blood pumping in Camille's ears drowned out what she was saying. She needed to get a hold of herself. Pulling her arm from Jenna's vise-like grip, she took a bite of quiche. It was just her luck. The most fuckable woman she'd met in well, forever, was ethically unfuckable. Camille sighed. She'd walked this line before with Mia and secrecy was not to her taste.

As if on cue, Hannah turned back to Camille and shot her a look that made her squirm in her chair. There was something so open in her expression that Camille couldn't do anything but smile back. She remembered how soft and sweet those lips had tasted against her own, the way they'd felt on her breasts. The spell was broken when Jenna slapped at her thigh like she'd seen a plague-ridden mosquito.

"Lady!" she hissed. "You guys are crushing so hard."

Camille couldn't deny it. "Yes, but she's a client."

"I'm sorry, what?" Melissa looked serious.

"I'm working on just one Gowear case. Helping out is all," Camille said, trying out the excuse.

Melissa wasn't buying it. "Be careful." The thoughtful brown eyes focused on her. "If they haven't formally announced the partnership yet..."

"I get it, Melissa. I need to play it safe." Camille huffed in frustration, but the doctor didn't take offense. Giving Camille a soft smile, she patted her arm.

Bonnie was now the only one at their table playing Bingo. She'd plucked Camille's card from the floor and was marking it along with her own as well as Melissa's and Jenna's.

"Anne fucking Heche!" she screamed, startling everyone.

"I hate that Draco-Malfoy-looking bitch," agreed a woman behind them.

"Right?" Bonnie picked up a pen and colored the Anne Heche box on each card so black the name was almost completely obscured.

"Will you go out with her?" Jenna whispered, picking up their conversation.

"It's tricky, Jenna."

"But you want to," Jenna persisted.

"Give her a break, baby," Melissa chided her wife.

Camille looked back at Hannah, laughing with Molly at the next trivia clue. Camille knew if Hannah dropped the microphone right now and asked her to leave the diner on the back of the Harley Davidson, she wouldn't hesitate. Her body responded as if everything had already been decided. An affair might invite professional risk, but smiling into Hannah's eyes, Camille had never felt safer.

The game came to a climax a few minutes later when a pink-haired millennial shouted "Bingo!" and ran to the front of the room to prove her case. A quick check of the scorecard confirmed she was indeed the winner. Afterward, Hannah posed for pictures with the starstruck young woman, Molly, and the Ellen cutout. Camille wondered if she would come to her table when free of obligations. Her question was answered when Hannah lifted her head and caught Camille's eye across the room. The smile told her everything. Hannah was definitely coming over. In fact, she was on her way right now.

There was an audible murmur in the restaurant as patrons watched Hannah thread her way toward Camille. If Hannah noticed, she didn't seem to care. She made no secret of her destination and Camille's heart soared at the sight of her approach. Seeing her again was like a shot of adrenaline. When Hannah reached the table, Camille rose from her chair and held out her arms like they were old friends. Hannah played along. Walking easily into Camille's embrace, she held her close, whispering into her ear.

"I'm so glad to see you." Her warm breath tickled Camille's skin, causing a flutter of arousal low in her core.

"Me too," Camille whispered back. Her body was now flushing with heat. Reluctantly, she pulled away. Remembering her manners, she addressed the table. "Ladies, this is Hannah."

CHAPTER TEN

Teahouse

The tiny teahouse over the sushi restaurant was empty. Camille couldn't determine if the lack of clientele was attributable to the odd time of day or if the establishment just reviewed poorly. There'd been no time to consult Yelp.

The crush of people in Molly's Diner had made it impossible for them to talk. It was also far too public. Jenna's woeful ignorance aside, the DC lesbian community was very much aware of who Hannah Richards was. The giddy young woman who'd won the trip to LA had live-streamed the presentation of the grand prize. When Molly had taken her picture with Hannah and the Ellen cutout, Camille thought the girl might faint.

Hannah's public declaration of her interest in Camille in front of eighty urban-professional lesbians was not the best way to keep their relationship under wraps. It was dangerous. But with Hannah next to her, Camille couldn't muster any anxiety. In fact, she couldn't remember ever feeling happier.

Hannah had utterly charmed Jenna and Melissa. The politically active couple were longtime supporters of Planned Parenthood and knew the value of Gowear's sponsorship. Ellen Trivia Bingo had raised more than fifteen thousand dollars for the local chapter. Hannah had downplayed her involvement, but after some prodding from Jenna she admitted to having secured the grand prize. She knew Ellen personally through the LGBT charity circuit. Bonnie had been suitably impressed with the connection but over the moon when Hannah had not only remembered Kathy, but also her love of root beer candy.

Camille met Hannah's friends on the way out. The small dark-haired woman was indeed Bree, Hannah's best friend from college and business partner at the climbing gym in Virginia. The blonde was Bree's girlfriend, Jane. The two made constant eye contact and were holding hands under the table. They reminded Camille of Jenna and Melissa. The older woman, a firecracker named Ruth, was as Bonnie had surmised, Jane's mother.

She'd accused Camille of bird-dogging her date, but there was a smile on her face. Jokes aside, none of the women had seemed the least bit surprised when Hannah had announced she and Camille were leaving. Bree had even made a surprising remark about having heard a lot about her. She'd said that she hoped to see Camille again soon. Had Hannah been talking about Camille to her friends? The thought made her light-headed.

A server had yet to appear, but they'd seated themselves in a cozy booth at the back of the tiny teahouse. It hardly seemed real. Camille had been thinking about Hannah all week, dreaming of her every night, feeling increasingly pessimistic about ever seeing her again. Now she was here, sitting across from her. The physical attraction Camille felt to Hannah was incredible. More incredible still was that Hannah was looking at Camille as if she felt exactly the same way. The beautiful golden eyes were following her like a cat watching a butterfly. It gave Camille a delicious feeling of anticipation. The action in Hannah's eyes foretold intent. The only thought in Camille's head was yes.

The teahouse was only three storefronts down from Molly's Diner but felt half a world away. Incense rose in the air and the rhythmic sound of chanting monks came from a speaker on the bar. Their booth, upholstered in a patterned hemp fabric, had matching pillows and headrests. It felt exotic and Camille was enchanted. Hannah reached across the table and took her hand. Twisting her fingers, she gave them a gentle squeeze. Incapable of resistance Camille gave herself over to the sensation of her touch. Sitting here, holding Hannah's hand, though she was a veritable stranger and now apparently a client, felt exactly like the place she needed to be.

Camille brushed her thumb over a small number one lightly scripted on Hannah's wrist.

"Lucky number?" she asked.

"I hope so." Hannah's lips tipped up in a sexy smile and her eyebrows rose in delight. Again, Camille noticed the small scar on the right side. She wanted to kiss it.

"I think it definitely is."

Hannah giggled and Camille wanted to kiss her lips, her neck. God, the woman was appealing. Happy, loose and languid, she exuded an easy sensuality that Camille wanted to dive into like a pool. She crossed her legs under the table and tried to focus on what Hannah was saying.

"One was my number in soccer. I played goalie for my college team. It was how I got into college, actually." Her voice took on a serious tone alerting Camille that there was more to the story. She resolved to ask her about it later. Should there be a later. God, she hoped there was a later. Camille paused her thumb on the tattoo.

"My birthday is January first."

"No fucking way."

"Yes. There's always a huge party, like it or not."

"I don't believe you," Hannah challenged, her voice a teasing sing-song.

"It's true."

Camille pulled out her driver's license and slid it across the table. Hannah studied it intently.

"You're so pretty. Even in this picture, you're pretty."

Camille blushed, but managed to maintain eye contact. "Thank you. For the record, I find you stunning."

"Thank you," Hannah said quietly. She handed the card back to Camille. "Why do you have a California driver's license?"

"Because I live in San Francisco."

"Oh." Her face fell a little, and Camille felt her heart do a small flip. She knew she was getting caught up in a flight-of-fancy, but somehow couldn't stop herself. She retook Hannah's hand and warmth spread from the point of contact up her arm like an electric current. Camille was reminded of being on the back of the Harley, the kiss by the river. Giving Hannah's hand a squeeze, she said what was on her mind.

"I had a great time the other night. The flying, the ride around the monuments, all of it."

Hannah's eyes sparkled at the memory. "I did too." She laced her fingers through Hannah's.

"I'm sorry my father's cats cut the night short."

They shared a shy smile, both thinking of what might have been.

"That's a wild scene you've got over there," Hannah said. "When I stopped by today, they rushed the door. The big one looked like she was out for blood."

"Did you really bring me flowers?"

Hannah squeezed her hand. "I wanted to see you."

"And here I am."

"Here you are."

Hannah licked her lips and smiled. God, Camille wanted to kiss her. To distract herself, she shared the story of Joe Robbins and the Kardashian cat family.

"He got all five cats on the same day?"

"Yes."

"How?"

"We still don't know."

"And that's why you're here from San Francisco?"

"Yes."

"To scoop litter boxes?"

"Pretty much." Camille hesitated. This was the time to tell Hannah about her job, come clean about the conflict of interest. "I'm also doing a little work."

"What do you do?"

"I'm a lawyer with Walker and Jenkins."

Camille waited for a reaction. From the blank look on Hannah's face, Walker and Jenkins could be a new Rob Lowe drama on Netflix.

"We represent Gowear. That's why I attended the party at the 9:30 Club. I work for you, Hannah. Technically, it's unethical for us to get involved."

The low throaty giggle that rolled across the table threatened to derail Camille's train of thought. Hannah squeezed her fingers, again.

"Don't worry, Camille. We don't have to try anything *too* technical, at least not on the first date. And Waldo Jennings doesn't need to know anything about us."

Us. The word made Camille blush. Hannah noticed and laughed even harder. It was as if she knew exactly how much the verbal foreplay was affecting Camille. Moving closer, she pressed her advantage. "Gowear is my father's company. You don't work for me. You work for my dad. I run a climbing gym in Virginia. That's where I go every day."

Hannah let go of Camille's hand and traced a finger up her arm, wrist to elbow. Waves of sensation flowed up toward Camille's shoulder. She knew she was going to give in, but first needed to clarify what she was giving in to.

"Bonnie told us you hold a half-interest in the company. I wouldn't ask, but it could affect my job."

Camille felt Hannah's body tense as she looked away.

"It's complicated." She paused, as if trying to decide something, and then began stroking Camille's arm once more.

"Yes, as far as Uncle Sam is concerned, I do own half the company. But I don't work there, and I certainly don't consider it mine." She hesitated again, and then continued. "A few years ago my dad got married. The woman, Stacey, is only a year older than me. You might remember her from the Gowear party. She was the bleach blond woman in the tiger-print jacket."

"I do remember her."

Hannah now had Camille's full attention. The derisive way she'd referenced Stacey was cause for concern. Though the Lulu Fabray settlement was only one signature away from being resolved, Camille still needed to be careful. Being privy to personal issues between Hannah and her stepmother, presumably two of Gowear's major shareholders, represented exactly the kind of impropriety Walker and Jenkins' no-fraternization rule was designed to prevent. So far, Hannah only knew Camille was working on a Gowear case. She didn't know which one. Camille decided to leave it that way.

She watched as Hannah tucked a strand of red hair behind her ear and rubbed at her nose. "Dad made me a fifty percent partner at Gowear to protect my inheritance, in case he and Stacey ever split up." She sighed. "I do some of the company's charitable outreach to make it legit."

"That sounds complicated."

Hannah looked validated. "Right? It was a generous thing for him to do, but it makes me feel beholden to him, and I don't like that. He and my mom were never married. We didn't even have a relationship until after she died."

Camille struggled to fill in the blanks. "When did your mom die?"

"Just before I finished college."

"I'm sorry," Camille said, and then added quietly, "My mom died too, about eight years ago."

Hannah took her hand again. "What happened? It's all right if you don't want to tell me."

"It's okay." Camille smiled sadly. Mary Robbins's untimely death was something Camille rarely talked about, but looking into Hannah's golden eyes, she wanted to share. "It was lung cancer."

"Oh, no."

"Yeah, it went really quickly—she died only four months after being diagnosed. One day she was playing tennis and the next hospice was moving in. I remember someone said it was a blessing. But it never felt like that to me, you know? My mother died. How was that a blessing?"

Hannah nodded. "I get it. My mom died in a car crash. She was killed instantly. Someone once told me that was a blessing and Bree had to hold me back."

"I thought your mom drove a motorcycle?"

"She was in her boss's car. He got out without a scratch."

"I'm sorry."

"Do you ever forget and want to call her?"

"All the time."

They shared a quiet moment and then Hannah began talking again.

"What's difficult is that Stacey goes overboard trying to build a relationship with me. The woman won't let up. She was the one who insisted I pose for the catalog cover."

Camille held up a hand. "Okay, that cover is hot. I won't hear a word against it."

"Thank you," Hannah blew out a breath, "but I didn't have a choice. When Stacey wants something, she's relentless. The crazy Gowear parties are all her too. Before Dad got married, Gowear had a crab feast at the wharf."

"Really?" Camille nodded politely. She didn't want to get into another conversation about Stacey Tabor.

Hannah nodded. "I think she may really love him. I know he adores her. She's just over-the-top, constantly buying him presents. Last week she came home with snakeskin boots. It wasn't even his birthday. On his birthday she had a surprise party with fifteen hundred guests."

"That's pretty impressive." Camille smiled. And undoubtedly the way Lulu Fabray had learned of the T-shirt.

"Are you worried that she's spending all his money?"

Hannah snorted. "Stacey loves to spend money. She's even richer than Dad. Did you know that? Texas hot sauce money." She smiled sheepishly.

"I had no idea."

"It's true. I don't know why I find her so annoying. The woman is not awful. She's just extra. Everything she touches is inflated, it kind of drives me crazy. Bree thinks we might have too much in common, and that really drives me crazy." Hannah frowned and Camille sought to put her at ease.

"You can't help who you click with."

"No, you can't."

Camille stretched her leg out and pressed her ankle against Hannah's calf. Hannah's eyes closed at the touch, a small smile playing on her lips. She toyed with Camille's fingers, bending her hand back and forth, as if testing their flexibility. Camille reveled in the attention. She was glad they were no longer talking about Stacey. She didn't want to talk at all. She ached for Hannah to touch her but knew they needed to get everything out in the open first. Hannah didn't need to know which Gowear case had created a conflict of interest, but she did need to understand the severity of getting caught.

"I'm on track for a partnership any day now. There's a possibility Walker and Jenkins would hold it up, if they found out we were spending time together."

"What? Why?" Hannah's flirty tone sobered considerably. She stopped playing with Camille's fingers.

"It would be considered a conflict of interest. They would say it was unethical."

"Well, that's not good." Hannah let Camille's hand go altogether. She did not break eye contact, though the golden light had dimmed to a faint glow.

Camille hesitated. If she was going to back out, this was the time to do it. But she didn't want to. The odds of anyone learning of their involvement and caring enough to make trouble were next to nothing. Mia was the only potential wildcard. The thought of her former lover thwarting a second of her personal happiness made Camille physically ill. Ultimately, this was the deciding factor. She chose her words carefully.

"The only not good thing I can imagine is if we didn't explore this attraction."

Hannah licked her lips, but her eyes remained full of concern.

"Are you sure?"

"Yes." Camille took the frog figurine out of her pocket and placed it on the table. "I found this today in my basement. I've decided to take it as sign."

Hannah brightened. She picked up the statue and musing, steered it around the table. "This guy was in your house? Frogme on a motorcycle?"

"Yes."

"And you've been carrying him around in your pocket all day?"

Camille bit her lip. "My friends say I conjured you up."

Hannah drove the frog across the table to Camille, then took her hand again. Relief at the renewed contact flooded through Camille's body like she'd just been let out of a speeding ticket. "I don't want to get you in trouble with Waldo Jennings."

Camille lifted her leg and placed it on Hannah's lap. "Waldo Jennings doesn't have to know anything."

Hannah dropped a hesitant hand to Camille's ankle. "If you're sure." Her fingers closed and then slid up Camille's calf, causing Camille to squirm.

"I am. But we won't have much time. I'm only here another few weeks." She tried to sound casual but heard her voice waver. For the second time that day she felt like she was in a movie. Hannah continued to stroke her leg, moving her long fingers up as far as they would reach, before dragging them back down again. Camille received the attention as if in a trance, while allowing herself a bold study of Hannah's face. Her eyes caressed the small scar, the flirty kissable lips. "We'll have to be very sneaky."

"We'll be the definition of stealth. Stealthy sex ninjas." Hannah was all mischief—so sexy that Camille wanted to begin right away.

"Seal the deal with a kiss?"

The golden eyes danced. "Right here, right now?" She tapped the index finger of her free hand on the table.

"Yes."

"In this booth?"

"Yes, please." There was something about being with Hannah that allowed Camille to speak her mind. "I don't want to wait." And it was true. Camille had no idea how long she'd be in DC. Why put off beginning what was already destined to be a brief interlude?

Hannah gently extracted Camille's foot from her lap and placed it on the floor. Lifting out of the booth, she swung to the other side, and pulled Camille snuggly against her. The press of her breasts against Camille's felt like heaven and Camille tilted her head up for the promised kiss. At first contact, Hannah slid her tongue into Camille's mouth, ratcheting the passion in an instant. The room began to fade, and for an indeterminate period, Camille lost all sense of place. She was only aware that her hand was inside Hannah's shirt when she felt the warm flesh of a breast in her hand. *God, what was she doing?* She started to pull away but Hannah grabbed her wrist.

"Don't stop."

For a heady moment, Camille did as she was told. Taking advantage of the privacy afforded by the empty restaurant, she gently stroked Hannah's breasts while continuing to kiss her face and neck. Hannah was so sexy; Camille's mind was on overload. She ached to take one of Hannah's nipples in her mouth. Hannah seemed to read her mind. Reaching up, she tugged down the neckline of her shirt, granting Camille both access and permission. Camille dropped her head and took the exposed nipple between her lips. She sucked it gently drawing a moan from Hannah. Camille felt her heart swell. Hannah tasted salty and smelled like baby shampoo. Camille teased the nipple with her lips and tongue. When Hannah moaned louder, Camille forced herself to stop.

"We can't do this here."

"Why not?" Hannah's body pulsed hotly against hers.

"It's a terrible way to begin a secret affair." Camille straightened the fabric of Hannah's bra and shirt. She looked up to meet golden eyes hazy with desire. "But we could go somewhere else."

"Where?" Hannah's voice was low and sexy. Camille fought the urge to pull her back in. "Do you have a place in mind?"

"Well, there are lots of cats at my dad's house…" Camille started but Hannah's kiss-stung lips finished the sentence for her.

"And zero cats at mine."

CHAPTER ELEVEN

Stealthy Sex Ninjas

The ride to Hannah's Dupont Circle townhouse was like an erotic fantasy. There was something undeniably hot about traveling to a specific destination with the express purpose of stripping a new lover naked and fucking them senseless. A vibrating purple motorcycle only made things more provocative. But Camille didn't need extrinsic accelerants. Merely thinking about Hannah's body was enough to quicken her pulse. She pushed herself back on the bike to ease the friction against her crotch. She needed to pace herself. Though Hannah had more than responded to the liberties Camille had taken in the teahouse, she doubted the redhead would be impressed if Camille dry-humped herself to orgasm on New Hampshire Avenue.

She tried to distract herself with the passing cityscape. The late nineteenth-century townhouses lining the avenue were beautiful. Made of locally mined limestone and brick, they created a timeless aesthetic that mirrored Camille's neighborhood in San Francisco. Over the decades, the formerly rundown area had been completely colonized by upscale young professionals. Each townhouse now had a perfectly manicured garden, framed by an ornate wrought-iron fence. It reminded Camille of the first row of a glorious, patchwork quilt.

Dupont Circle was named for the traffic circle that connected residential DC to downtown and was known for having a large LGBT population. Each year, in the spring, it hosted the Capital Pride Parade, and at Halloween, a drag race that had nothing to do with cars.

Hannah pulled the Harley into a parking space in front of a magnificent gray, stone townhouse. Camille peered up at the elegant building with the covered front porch and turreted tower, and guessed it was built around 1900. Her place in San Francisco dated a little older at 1890.

"Is this you?"

"That's my girl."

"She's really beautiful."

"I can't take any credit. I bought her fully renovated." Hannah dismounted the bike and offered a hand to Camille. Long fingers wrapped easily around her elbow, keeping her steady as she slid to the sidewalk. When Camille was safely on the ground, the fingers did not let go, but crept higher on her arm.

"I wish I was one of those hot carpenter chicks. But growing up with just my mom we weren't very handy. I swear there wasn't a tool in our whole house. If we needed a screwdriver she used a butter knife." She lightly stroked Camille's bicep.

"But your mom drove a motorcycle," Camille said and smoothed her hand across the seat of the Harley, "how could she not be handy?"

"No one touched this baby but the guy at the shop. That's why she's still in such good condition." Hannah squeezed Camille's shoulder.

"So you had to become a hot soccer chick instead?" Camille heard her voice hitch, and knew she sounded like a teenager. But how was she expected to be cool when her body was on fire?

"It was the only other option," Hannah said and continued to touch her, lightly running her fingers up and down her arm.

The two women stood smiling at each other on the sidewalk as Camille struggled to maintain control of her hands. She was still so turned on from the make-out session in the tearoom that she could barely look at Hannah without risking a move that could get them arrested for public indecency.

"I'm not handy either," she said nervously, "I've hired a contractor to renovate my townhouse in San Francisco. He hates me because I live in the basement and harass him relentlessly."

"That sounds kind of fun to me." Hannah looked at her intently.

Camille met her bold stare, and almost lost her train of thought. "I'm learning a lot," she whispered. In an effort to regain control, she turned and looked at Hannah's garden. Enclosed by an intricate wrought-iron fence, the small space was planted with interwoven ivy. The result was a beautiful, verdant maze.

Camille was impressed. Her last garden had been a pathetic display of a few spindly perennials. She'd kept them alive for exactly two seasons, whereupon they'd died a sad death of neglect.

"Your garden is amazing."

Hannah gave her a sparkly smile. "It came with the house." She pointed over the gate at the clean lines of the patterned ivy. "The previous owner designed the maze. It was his art."

Camille paused at the top of the steps and looked down at the miniature labyrinth. "It's really beautiful. Do you maintain it yourself?"

"No!" Hannah looked horrified. "I pay a service, like a million dollars a month." She lifted a round knob on top of the gate. Swinging it open, she stood aside to let Camille pass through first.

"The former owner moved around the corner. He walks his dogs by here every morning. I can't let him down."

"Oh no." Camille stopped short. "That sounds like a hostage situation."

Hannah took the opportunity to snake her long fingers around Camille's waist, pulling her body against her own. Camille was reminded of Hannah's slight height advantage, and how much she liked it.

"Yes, and it's way too much pressure." Her voice was warm and low in Camille's ear, her breasts firm against her back.

"Pressure is not always a bad thing," Camille managed to say, and was rewarded with the throaty giggle that made her knees weak.

She reached out for the stone railing to steady herself, and a carved face above the entrance caught her eye. "Who's that?"

"Albus," Hannah hissed the soft S against Camille's neck, causing her to shudder. "I think it's supposed to be Zeus, but I changed it. I like the stories better."

"Me too," Camille murmured. She leaned back into the warm body behind her. "Why are we whispering?"

Hannah's answer was immediate. "Because it's sexier."

"Do you think we need help?"

Hannah tightened her grip on Camille but otherwise didn't answer. They stood there allowing additional heat to collect between them. When Hannah finally spoke again, her voice was hoarse. "Do you want to go inside?"

"Yes," Camille said the word, and knew it was the answer to any question Hannah might ask her.

She stood on shaky legs as Hannah unlocked the big wooden door and then followed her inside the house. Camille caught only a peripheral view of the foyer, before warm lips crashed against her own. At the contact, pure happiness surged through Camille's body. The pleasure was so intense that her brain completely turned off, and she succumbed to the sensation of being well and truly kissed. Her whole world became Hannah's hot, wet mouth, her probing, stroking tongue. Food-sex metaphors popped into her mind. She wanted to consume, devour, ravish Hannah. Pick a word. She couldn't get enough.

Suddenly, her back was against something solid, and Hannah's strong hands were in her hair, holding her carefully in place. They slipped to her breasts and boldly thumbed her nipples through the fabric of her shirt.

All the while she continued to kiss her. Her lips fused so tightly to Camille's that, for the first time, she understood the expression lip-lock. Hardware would be required to separate them.

When Hannah finally pulled away she was panting for air.

"Damn, Camille," she whispered, breathing hard, "you're fucking killing me." It was only then that Camille realized her hand was inside Hannah's jeans.

"Oh my God. I'm so sorry." Camille was shocked by her own behavior. When Hannah was nearby her hands seemed to move of their own accord. They went where they wanted to go, touched what they wanted to touch. First in the teahouse and now in the entrance hall. It was fortunate Hannah was so responsive. She started to pull away but Hannah pressed into her.

"Don't you dare," she hissed, and leaned in harder, increasing the pressure against her center. Camille felt the heat of Hannah's arousal slick against her palm, and almost came undone herself. She slid a finger inside her and felt the walls of her core contract. Hannah was right on the edge.

"What do you need?" Camille closed her teeth over Hannah's ear and bit down lightly. She flicked her tongue inside and Hannah gasped.

"Oh God, just kiss me. Please?"

Her voice was so soft, and full of need that Camille felt tears sting the back of her eyes. Emotion surged through her. She pressed up into another searing kiss and slid a second finger inside Hannah causing her to jerk up. Breaking the kiss, she cried out. Then locking eyes with Camille, she rocked her hips against her hand, as she rode out the release. It was the sexiest thing Camille had ever seen, and she gasped in surprise to experience a smaller orgasm of her own.

Hannah gave her a hesitant smile. "Did you just get off, watching me get off?"

"I did." Camille gently slid her fingers from Hannah's warm center. Without thinking, she brought them to her lips to lick them clean.

"Lady," Hannah said the word reverently. "What is going on here?" She wrapped her long arms around Camille and pulled her into a snug embrace.

"We're having sneaky, stealth-ninja sex," Camille said into her hair. She knew it sounded like a class at the gym offered after Zumba, but what was the alternative? Telling Hannah that after two weeks' acquaintance she felt a connection full of promise and potential, didn't seem the way to go.

"Well, it's amazing," Hannah said candidly. She rubbed her breasts back and forth against Camille's, causing electric shocks of pleasure to shoot straight to her groin. Camille pushed her hips forward reflexively and Hannah giggled low into her neck. The throaty sound made Camille nearly mad with desire and she whimpered in frustration.

Hannah stopped moving. Cradling Camille's face in her hand, she smiled sweetly into her eyes. "Don't worry. We're nowhere near done."

She took Camille's hand and pulled her forward. Camille didn't ask where they were going. She hoped it was Hannah's bed, but knew she would settle for any horizontal surface away from the windows if it meant Hannah could be fucking her sooner.

They passed through the spacious foyer and into a central hallway bathed pale blue from a stained glass skylight. Beneath their feet, one-hundred-year growth heart-of-pine floors were enhanced by a sumptuous Turkish carpet in rich jewel tones. Off the foyer, to the right, a spacious room with a bay window looked out onto the street. The back wall was scalloped like a pie plate and a long Mission-style table and six chairs were centered on a Persian Quashqui rug.

Everywhere Camille looked there was evidence of taste and care. In a room to the left, plants spilled from wrought iron stands on either side of an elaborate fireplace. Framed prints of old maps flanked the green-tiled mantel and the portrait of a Native American woman made Camille want to ask Hannah questions. But strong fingers pulled her on. The time for questions would come later. There were other things they needed to discover first.

They reached the foot of an ornately carved wooden staircase, and Hannah tugged her forward. Camille wondered if she could feel her heart beating against her palm. Six steps up, and Hannah spun her around and pressed their lips together.

Camille gave in for a hot minute, before pushing her away. "Stop it." She hissed, but then kissed her again, harder.

"I don't want to stop," Hannah huffed against Camille's mouth. She took her hand again, and somehow they were on the second floor. Camille trailed her down a long hallway. A door stood open at the end. Surely, there was a bed inside. Camille couldn't wait much longer. She licked her lips and caught the residual essence of Hannah on her tongue.

"Oh God," she whispered, savoring the taste.

Hannah hadn't bothered to refasten her jeans. They hung low on her hips, waiting for Camille to push them down again. Entering the room, she turned to face Camille.

"Is something wrong?" There was the smallest hint of uncertainty in her normally confident voice. Did Hannah really think Camille would reject her now? Camille found the idea ludicrous and almost laughed but caught the vulnerable expression in Hannah's eye and stopped short.

"Nothing is wrong," she said firmly, and then glanced purposefully behind Hannah to the king-sized bed. In the middle of the room, covered in a thick white duvet, the bed set Camille's imagination alight with possibilities.

Hannah extended her hand. "I'm glad." The relief in her voice filled Camille with tenderness. She caught a tantalizing glimpse of Hannah's white, lace thong and licked her lips. She leaned in to kiss her.

Hannah met her halfway and they began a series of long slow, kisses that made Camille's body hum with pleasure. She desperately wanted to lie down on top of Hannah, press against her heat. But when she moved forward, Hannah put out a hand to stop her. Her voice was soft. "Will you undress for me?"

"Okay." Camille swallowed hard, and stepped back nervously. Maintaining eye contact, she leaned over to remove her shoes and socks. Next came her pants and T-shirt. Standing in her matching green bra and panties, she allowed Hannah to look at her.

The verdict came quickly. "You're gorgeous." She pulled Camille into her arms and they tumbled onto the bed, Camille on top. Wasting no time, Hannah slipped her hands inside Camille's underwear. Cupping her ass, she squeezed it gently and let her fingers drift lower toward Camille's slit.

"I thought you wanted me to undress for you." Camille choked and was met with a lick up the side of her neck.

"I decided to help," Hannah whispered in her ear. "I'm nice that way." In one deft movement, she yanked down Camille's panties and slid them over her feet. Next she unsnapped the bra and pushed it aside. Just like that, Camille was completely naked.

She gasped. "Thank you."

"It's my pleasure." Hannah's hands began moving at random across Camille's body. She felt them in her hair as Hannah kissed her face and neck. They were on her breasts, kneading the soft underswells and pulling at her nipples. And, finally, they were between her legs, stroking her wet folds. Dipping inside, Hannah teased her. Never giving her quite enough, she stoked her need for more. Camille leaned into every caress. She was desperate to find a rhythm to pace her release, but Hannah continued to play. Lazily she built her up. Stroking the length of Camille from behind she slipped a second finger inside her.

"You're so wet," she whispered. Her voice was sweet, and she pushed in her fingers more deeply. Camille lifted her herself off the bed to allow better access. She was now on all fours, legs spread shamelessly astride Hannah's body. She rocked her hips hard against Hannah's hand, and her breasts swung over her face. The redhead caught a nipple in her mouth and sucked hard before turning her attention to the other. The pleasure was exquisite and Camille cried out. She pushed harder into the fingers, careening quickly toward the edge. Hannah pumped her hand faster, and Camille exploded.

"Hannah, Hannah, Hannah, Hannah, Hannah," Camille breathed the name through her release like it was a mantra. She knew it was an admission of sorts, but she didn't care. Something special was happening here.

Hannah softened her strokes, and then pulled out entirely. Camille whimpered in protest and then felt strong hands gripping the backs of her thighs.

"Hold onto the headboard," she commanded, and pulled Camille's still-contracting pussy toward her lips.

"Hannah!" Camille screamed the name this time. Gripping the back of the bed as instructed, her body began to shake as Hannah sucked as much of her into her mouth as possible. Her long tongue slipped in and around Camille's dripping core, seemingly everywhere at once. Fanning the embers of Camille's desire, she built her up again. The next orgasm took her hard and fast. More powerful than the last, it detonated between them, causing Camille to scream Hannah's name yet again.

"I'm sorry, I'm sorry, I'm so sorry," she apologized, unabashedly riding out her climax against Hannah's face. It wasn't until several seconds later that she was able to detach herself completely. As she moved away, Hannah swiped her tongue a last time through her throbbing center. The intimacy felt profound. Given the newness of the relationship the tender emotions Camille experienced frightened her. Hannah's vulnerability inspired Camille to feel something beyond the intense physical attraction. It was a one-two combination that knocked Camille out.

She collapsed into a child's pose on top of Hannah and took several deep breaths. Warm hands that minutes earlier had been gripping her thighs in passion, moved to glide along her back. Hannah began to trace lazy lines down her spine, and Camille sighed into her chest. Holding this woman against her body felt undeniably correct. There was a safety in her arms she couldn't explain. They lay there for several moments catching their breath. Hannah was the first to speak.

"Why did you apologize?"

Camille kissed the space between Hannah's breasts. What was the point of openly acknowledging the effect Hannah had on her? Saying the words out loud would only make the feeling more powerful. Perhaps create a greater potential to hurt them both. She hedged with a lesser truth. "Because I made so much noise."

Hannah giggled and Camille's stomach flipped. "I love that you're so loud. It's totally sexy." She played with Camille's hair, combing the long blond strands through her fingers. "Do you know what else I think was really hot?"

"What?"

"The way you said my name." Hannah was not shy about addressing the issue. "The way you screamed my name actually." Her hands continued to play with Camille's hair. "I've seen people do that in movies, but it's the first time it's ever really happened to me." She confessed this easily. It felt like a gift, and Camille was compelled to reciprocate in kind.

"Well, I've never done it before," she replied. "But it shouldn't be a surprise. I've been thinking about you all week."

Hannah locked her arms tightly around Camille's body, and pressed her lips against her ear. "I'm really glad to hear that. Because I've been thinking about you too." Gently, she bit down on the lobe. Camille felt fresh heat gather in her center, and knew the afternoon wasn't over.

CHAPTER TWELVE

Aftergloat

Spending the night in Hannah's bed wasn't an option. In addition to the fact that Hannah hadn't formally invited her, Camille didn't want to stay out all night without giving her father advanced warning. Especially when her only excuse was more mind-blowing sex. Camille knew she and Hannah would have fucked again if she'd slept over. She knew this because Camille would've been the instigator. She simply could not keep her hands off the sexy redhead. The instinct to touch her was unprecedented. Camille hadn't realized she was fingering her in the foyer, until Hannah had almost come in her hand.

It was more than just pent-up lust from staring at the Gowear catalog cover and it was more than a little frightening. Their connection felt wild and organic, like a bolt of lightning. It was dangerous because Camille had no control over it. This also made it incredibly hot. Camille knew they shouldn't be involved at all. The minute Bonnie had informed her that Hannah was the heiress apparent at Gowear, Camille should've cut bait and run. Putting her partnership in jeopardy for short-term sex, no matter how earth-shattering, was stupid. But somehow— maybe it was driving around the city of her youth on the back of Hannah's Harley—the liaison had become a gift Camille wanted to give herself. And, after holding onto the headboard and coming hard against Hannah's face, she knew she owed herself a thank-you note.

The rest of the afternoon had been a continuous carnal interlude. Hannah had made Camille scream her name several times more, and Camille had happily returned the favor until they were both too tired to do anything but cuddle and chat. They'd stayed in Hannah's bed until nearly seven p.m., when Camille had reluctantly pried herself away and took an Uber back to Woodley Park. Hannah had offered to drive her home, but Camille needed time to collect herself before facing her father. Grinding herself to another orgasm on the back of the bike would not be the best way to accomplish this goal.

Joe Robbins could certainly survive the night without Camille's assistance but he deserved some notice. It was only fair. Martina had solved the catnip issue by insisting Joe stop giving the cats the drug altogether. Cold turkey. As a healthcare worker she was affronted by the blatant overdosing and had implied she might stop lingering after their physical therapy sessions if Joe didn't stop indulging the cats. In the end, her Bolognese sauce combined with a promise to assist in the detox effort had won the day. Poor Joe. For two days, the cats had pestered him constantly. They'd mewed in his face for hours on end hoping to score a fix. It hadn't stopped until he'd downloaded a rape whistle app on his own phone.

Now the situation was much improved though still imperfect. The cats no longer bothered Joe but had become hyperalert to any movement involving the front door. The minute any footfall was detected outside, they aggressively rushed the entrance. Camille had started keeping an old tennis racket in the umbrella stand. Martina had been philosophical.

"Of course they watch the door," she'd explained, and gestured around Joe's office. "There are no cat drugs in the house. If cat drugs are to come inside this house, how are they getting here?" She'd pointed to the stately oak-paneled entranceway. "They come through the drug door. These Kardashian cats are lazy but they are not stupid."

Hours earlier Martina had left to meet a friend at the National Gallery of Art. Thankfully, she'd prepared pesto gnocchi and left it in the refrigerator to be reheated for dinner. Camille was starving. Though she'd paid over two hundred dollars for the benefit brunch, she'd been too affected by Hannah's presence to eat more than a few bites. She'd polished off the gnocchi and half a loaf of bread before going back to look for ice cream. If her father noticed the uncharacteristic appetite he hadn't let on. Just as he hadn't asked her why Ellen Trivia Bingo Brunch had lasted eight hours.

Camille knew that if her mother were alive, she would've wondered about both anomalies. She would've prodded each situation carefully, never pushing, but nudging just enough. And then, when Camille was ready to talk, she would have listened. That was the thing Camille missed most. The comfort of knowing someone was paying attention to your life. Mary Robbins had asked Camille the hard questions, helped her sort out the messy truths. It always surprised Camille when friends complained about their parents being too focused on their lives. It was a trait she'd valued highly in her mother. Mary's worry had shifted some of the burden from Camille. Now Camille paid a therapist a lot of money to provide the same service.

Joe Robbins's seeming lack of curiosity didn't upset his daughter. Camille knew he was game to talk about anything if she introduced the subject first. It was the unspoken rule of their relationship. Camille had always found the arrangement perfectly civilized. She got the benefit of a sympathetic ear without the annoyance of a presumptive tongue. Her father would never ask her directly why she'd come home six hours late, stinking of sex and hungrier than a college freshman on

Thanksgiving break. But if she wanted to talk about it, he'd clear his schedule.

On the other hand, Cory, like Jenna, was an aggressive information seeker. But Cory was stalking Lulu Fabray in Arizona. He was supposed to check in with Camille the next day at noon. Until he missed the deadline she would not allow herself to worry.

It was exhausting enough dealing with Jenna. By the time Camille had climbed into the Uber of Shame she'd already messaged Camille six times. Camille had promised to call her at nine p.m. with a full debrief. It was currently ten minutes before the hour.

She rose from the chair and collected her bowl of ice cream from the coffee table. Maybe confiding in Jenna would help her to understand her feelings better regarding Hannah. Physically, things were copacetic. Her body reacted as if it had found its perfect match. Hannah knew precisely how to touch her, make her come. Never before had Camille so completely lost herself in the now with no thought of past or future. Camille wanted to kiss Hannah for hours, sink into her very essence.

But it was more than just physical. They laughed together. Hannah was great company and surprisingly sweet. It felt like a true connection. Camille knew how rare this was. She certainly didn't have it with Val who rarely talked at all and had certainly never made Camille laugh. Wouldn't it be shortsighted to squander a shot at something real because of a conflict of interest that would disappear in a few days? What if this was her last chance?

She took her father's plate and stacked it on top of her own. Picking up his water glass, she smiled down at him fondly. He was binge watching a BBC miniseries and wouldn't miss Camille if she retired for the evening.

"Can I get you anything?"

Such was his focus that it took him a while to disengage his attention from the television. "I'm sorry, what?"

His eyes were tired, but his face looked relaxed. The convalescence was going well. Martina had ramped up the physical therapy. Joe would be fit enough to move back upstairs in a week or so. Camille could go back to San Francisco as soon as they could hire someone to clean the litter boxes. The Kardashians successfully detoxed, her father was no longer at risk of being reported to the ASPCA.

"I'm going to bed, Dad. Can I get you anything?"

"Just a glass of water, please."

"Sure."

Balancing the dinner plates, Camille bumped the kitchen door open with her hip. She was looking forward to recounting the events of her afternoon to Jenna. Sharing the story, saying the words out loud, would make the afternoon seem more real. As it stood, Camille could barely believe it had happened at all.

She put the plates into the sink and turned on the water. It was silly to dwell on it. Whatever she and Hannah were exploring would end when Camille left DC. Professional conflict aside, they lived at opposite sides of the continent. It would be naive to expect anything more than a few stolen interludes. Cory would tell her to enjoy it while it lasted.

She walked back into Joe's office where her father was now petting Kim and Kourtney. The cats sat on either side of the futon, receiving head and neck massages, while Joe Robbins kept an eye on the TV. Camille handed her father the water glass and picked up a dirty coffee cup. The phone rang in her pocket, and she rolled her eyes. Jenna was five minutes early.

"It's Jenna," she explained to Joe. "She's going to give me a hard time about this afternoon."

"Do you deserve one?"

The phone rang again. Once more, and it would go to voice mail. Camille winked at her father. "Possibly."

She put down the coffee cup and, pulling the phone from her pocket, answered it without looking. "Can't you wait five minutes?" She smiled at her father. For some reason she was pleased for him to see this normal interaction with Jenna.

Teasing a friend on the phone wasn't exactly a heart-to-heart chat, but it was a form of sharing. Something she hoped to do more of.

That thought, and all others, left her mind when she realized who was on the other end of the line. The low throaty, giggle instantly transported her back to Hannah's bedroom.

"Sure. I can wait five minutes. Do you want to call me back?" Hannah's voice was lazy and Camille imagined her propped up amongst the white pillows.

"Hannah!" The word came out in a rush. Joe must have noticed but, true to nature, he didn't let on. Turning politely away from Camille, he focused instead on the screen.

"Yes, Camille?" There was a smile in her voice.

"Please don't hang up."

"I won't."

Camille hurried into the dining room and shut the door. Since returning from Hannah's, she'd walked by many times to admire the flowers dropped off earlier in the day. A vibrant spring sampler of peonies, dahlias, and garden roses, they were obviously meant to impress. Martina had arranged them expertly in Mary Robbins's Waterford crystal vase and put them in the center of the table.

Cradling the phone against her ear, Camille said what had been on her mind since leaving Hannah's bed.

"I'm sorry I had to go. I mean, leave your house."

"Me too."

"Really?" Camille's heart did a small flip. Though Hannah's body language had communicated as much, she'd not actually said the words.

"Of course I am," she confessed easily. "The only reason I didn't tie you to the bed was because I knew you had to check on your dad. How is he, by the way?" Hannah pivoted neatly from the admission to a question.

"He's fine—great, actually. We just finished dinner and I was headed up to bed to call Jenna. I thought you were her."

"Do you need to go? We can talk later." Camille heard what sounded like the rustling of sheets and knew her assumption had been correct. Hannah was still in bed. Heat flooded her neck and down her chest as Hannah continued to speak. "I was just missing you and wanted to tell you that."

Camille jumped in quickly. "That's okay. I can call her later."

"Is Jenna the woman I met at Molly's today? The tiny brunette who works with you at Walker and Jenkins?"

"Good memory, yes. She's also an old friend who is very anxious to hear about my afternoon."

"Tell me about your afternoon, Camille." Hannah's voice was silky and Camille closed her eyes. Recalling the events of the day in detail, she felt the warmth creep lower.

"It was amazing."

"Tell me your favorite part? You tell me yours. I'll tell you mine."

"Okay."

Camille considered possible answers. The make out session in the tearoom had certainly been a highlight, as had the episode in Hannah's foyer and the all the activity in the big white bed. There was simply no way to narrow it down to a single event, so she decided to go with something general.

"Touching your beautiful body. I liked that."

"I liked that too. I really liked that."

"I'm glad, because I don't seem to have much control over my hands when you're near me."

"If it becomes a problem, I'll let you know."

"Okay, great." Camille touched a flower in the bouquet with the tip of her finger. "What was your favorite part?"

"That's easy. When you held on to the headboard and came in my mouth."

Camille put a hand on the table to steady herself. "Yeah, that was nice."

"I can still taste you. You know?"

"Hannah, you have no idea..."

"When can I see you again?"

The directness of Hannah's question made Camille's heart soar.

"Anytime, really. I want to see you too."

"Is tomorrow too soon?"

"Tomorrow is perfect. But we have to keep it private because…"

"Waldo Jennings, I know. Fuck him, he's not invited. I want to cook for you."

"You cook?"

"Come over tomorrow night and find out."

"Okay."

"Okay?"

Camille was surprised to hear a faint note of surprise in her voice. Was there ever a doubt she'd say yes?

"Yes. I'd love to come over for dinner tomorrow night."

"Great. Any dietary restrictions?"

"No."

"I'll see you at seven."

"Okay, and Hannah?"

"Yes?"

"Thank you for the flowers. They're beautiful." Camille stroked the soft underside of a petal and thought of Hannah's skin. "I can't remember the last time anyone sent me flowers."

"Well, now you can."

Hanging up, Camille blinked happily at the phone. Hannah wanted to see her again. In less than twenty-four hours, Camille would be back in her arms. She felt light-headed, floaty, like the time the oral surgeon had given her nitrous oxide. Except this time, the procedure she was anticipating wasn't a root canal.

The phone buzzed in her hand and she fantasized it was Hannah again, calling back to tell her tomorrow was too far away, that Camille should come over right now. But the screen identified the caller as Jenna. Right on schedule.

Before Camille could answer, the doorbell rang. It was nine p.m. on a Sunday night. Who could possibly be at the front door? If Martina had forgotten something, she would have called.

The bell rang again, and Camille started for the foyer. Her father was now capable of opening the front door but doing it while fending off drug-starved cats was another story.

"I'm coming," she shouted, moving quickly down the hallway. The cats were swirling around the front entrance in what looked to be some sort of cultish dance. Her father was yelling something from the other room, while trying to push himself off the futon and onto his crutches.

"Dad!" Camille ran to help him.

"Why are you getting up?"

The doorbell rang again, this time followed by a light knocking. Whoever it was wasn't going away.

Joe ran a hand through his thinning gray hair. "Because it's Sunday night and we're not expecting visitors."

It was a fair answer. Woodley Park may be a nice neighborhood, but it was still in the city, and they needed to be careful.

"Let me see who it is."

"I'm not sure that's a good idea."

"Don't worry, the cats will protect me." Camille walked quickly back into the foyer. The doorbell rang one more time. She stuck her eye to the peephole and her head snapped back in surprise.

"Jesus Christ."

"I certainly wasn't expecting him," Joe quipped.

Camille took the tennis racquet from the umbrella stand and brushed back the cats. "I'll only be a minute." Without waiting for a response, she pulled open the door and slipped out into the night.

CHAPTER THIRTEEN

Scotch Guard

"What are you doing here, Lillian?" Camille was direct. If something had happened to impact the Fabray settlement, she needed to know about it immediately. Too much was at stake. In her fondest dreams Cory would call her tomorrow and say the FedEx was in the mail. But until that happened—until the conflict of interest was resolved—until her partnership was safe—Camille had to be vigilant.

"I need to talk to you."

"Is it about the case?"

"No."

Lillian had been sulking around the office all week. But now, standing on the front stoop of Camille's childhood home in her ridiculous giraffe heels and perfectly tailored suit, she looked almost angry.

Camille gripped the Andre Agassi signature tennis racquet more tightly. "But you thought it was appropriate to come to my father's home, on a Sunday night?"

"Well, you're obviously not sleeping." The intelligent green eyes narrowed at the racquet. "Did I catch you on the way out?"

Camille held up the cat sweeper. "Yes, I was on my way to a tennis match in 1992. What do you want?"

"I want to talk to you about Mia."

"I'm sorry?"

"Mi-a." Lillian said the name again. This time it sounded like a karate cry.

Camille took an instinctive step back. "What about her?"

"Are you sleeping with her?"

"What? God, no." Camille heard the venom in her own voice, and cringed.

"But you were." It was not a question.

Camille sucked in a breath. Part of her wanted to be honest, if only to do the younger woman a service. She hated thinking someone else was being manipulated by Mia. The idea was despicable. But the minute she opened her mouth, she'd become involved—an equally despicable thought. Self-preservation won out. "It's none of your business."

"I knew it," Lillian said softly. She wobbled on her heels until Camille broke the silence.

"Why are you here? Why are you asking me this now?"

Lillian shook her head but didn't open her mouth. There was a slight tremor in her bottom lip that Camille recognized as the universal "about-to-cry" tell. One question regarding Lillian's emotional state, and the tears would flow. Camille hesitated and then, because Lillian's pained expression was the same one she used to see in the mirror, she posed the fatal question. "Is everything okay?"

Lillian shook her head again. "No. No, it's not. But we're not talking about that, are we?" The forecasted tears began to flow. Lillian let them go unchecked, as if they were an everyday occurrence.

"Lillian, please understand."

Lillian held up her hand like a crossing guard. "Mia asked me to tell you something. She wants you in New York. On

Tuesday. With her." She broke the directive into separate pieces like it was a pill too big to swallow whole. "Pack a bag, you're staying at the Soho Grand."

"What?"

"My lover wants you in New York." Despite the tears Lillian's voice stayed even.

"Lillian, stop this. Tell me what's going on."

"Another Gowear issue. Some hassle involving a wetsuit. Way above my pay grade, apparently. Mia wants you on it."

Camille was stunned. "But I can't start another Gowear project. I'm going back to California, maybe next week."

"That's not the intel coming back from the partners' meeting."

"What are you talking about, what intel?"

"That you're moving back to DC."

"What?"

Lillian stared hard at Camille. "Mia has lobbied to make the terms of your partnership contingent on you being based in Washington."

"That's not possible." All the spite in Camille's head flew out of her mouth like a flock of angry birds. "She is such a fucking bitch. How dare she try to control my life again! I can't believe this. Wait…" She was stopped short by the look of despair on Lillian's face. "How do you know what happened at the partners' meeting?"

Lillian grimaced but didn't speak at first as the tears fell. When she found her voice, it was small. "Mia told me."

Camille shook her head. None of this made any sense. "But why? Why would she do that?"

"She's trying to push me away by pretending she wants to be with you. We're getting too close, and she can't handle it."

"Oh, Lillian." Camille wanted to squeeze her arm but thought better of it. Lillian might not be receptive to a comforting touch from her perceived rival. Despite her emotional state, she seemed to have a clear read on the situation. The partnership stunt and the effect it was clearly having on Lillian was completely in keeping with Mia's preference for emotional distance. "I'm sorry she's doing this. I truly am. But I'm not involved with her and I don't want to become involved with her. I promise."

"I believe you. I apologize for interrupting your evening." Once again the green eyes filled with tears. She turned to go, but the abrupt twist of her heel caused her shoe to snap and she began to fall backward down the steps. Camille caught her just in time, pulling her upright.

"Careful!"

Lillian shrugged out of Camille's grasp, but stepped up on the landing next to her. Removing the broken stiletto from her foot, she flung it down the stairs where it clattered to the sidewalk. It must have been satisfying, as she then repeated the action with the other shoe. The second shoe went farther. Careening into the street, it was run over by a passing minivan. The violence of the act shocked both of the women into silence. After a moment, Lillian muttered. "I hate those fucking shoes."

Camille began to laugh. "Yeah, I guess so."

In her stocking feet, Lillian was now eye level with Camille. She was no longer crying but tear tracks were still visible on her cheeks. "I'm sorry I bothered you at your father's house on a Sunday. I'll see you tomorrow."

She took the first step toward the sidewalk.

"Wait," Camille had no idea what she would say, but sending Lillian out into the night with a tear-streaked face and no shoes, did not seem like an option.

"What?"

"Do you want to come inside?"

"I thought you didn't want to talk."

"Maybe I changed my mind."

"Maybe?"

Camille cracked opened the door. "At least let me find you a pair of flip-flops."

"Okay."

Batting Kardashians away with the Agassi racquet, Camille created enough space for Lillian to enter the house. The second the door closed, the cats began twisting around Lillian's ankles, pawing at her purse.

"What's the matter with these cats?"

"They're looking for drugs," Joe called out helpfully from the other room.

"What?" Lillian pulled up the strap of her purse, unseating Rob who'd somehow managed to position himself atop the wide Coach tote like it was a hammock. The male cat landed on Kim, who responded with characteristic histrionics, letting out such a banshee wail that the rest of the family scattered. Lillian shrieked in fright.

"Oh my God, I'm so sorry." With the tennis racquet, Camille nudged the cats away from Lillian and ushered her into Joe's office. Let her father explain his pets.

"Dad, this is Lillian. She's a lawyer at Walker and Jenkins."

Her father sat up on the futon and extended his hand. If Joe noticed any resemblance to Lillian and Camille's younger self, he didn't let on. The stocking-foot young associate moved forward to meet him.

"Joe Robbins. The cats are entirely my fault. Camille has nothing to do with them. I promise. She's not the crazy cat person. I am." The gleam in his eye told Camille that he thought Lillian might be the reason she'd been detained at brunch.

"Dad, Lillian stopped by to tell me about an upcoming work trip."

Joe raised an eyebrow, clearly wondering why the news required a personal visit.

"I broke my heel," Lillian explained.

Joe nodded knowingly. "Camille wore high heels when she got out of law school. Her mother said she was role-playing *LA Law*."

"I was not," Camille protested. "And I don't even know what that is."

"She wore these fancy suits too. Very la-ti-da. Spent all her money on clothes."

Lillian smirked at Camille. "I bet she did."

Camille sighed. "Do you need anything Dad? Lillian and I are going to talk in the kitchen."

Joe waved them away. The Kardashians had settled themselves on various perches in the cat condo. Though still keeping an eye on the front door, they seemed calm.

"I'm fine. Thank you, love. It was nice meeting you Lillian. Hope you two have a nice talk."

"Dad."

Joe ignored his daughter. "And it's okay with me if you want to spend the night. Camille's friends are always welcome."

Lillian looked surprised. "Thank you, Mr. Robbins, but I won't be staying that long."

Camille glared at her father. "We work together."

"The flowers are beautiful by the way," Joe continued, referencing Hannah's exquisite bouquet.

"Lillian did not send me flowers, Dad."

There was an awkward silence, and then Joe cleared his throat. "Oh, well they're quite lovely."

Lillian eyed Camille. "I'm sure they are."

Camille ushered Lillian into the kitchen to a seat at the table.

"Your dad's sweet."

"He's obnoxious."

"And you're gay."

"Excuse me?"

"I said, you're gay."

"Why do you say that?"

"Well, your fingernails were my first clue, but your father clearly just thought I was your lover. That kind of gave it away."

"It's not a secret."

"Maybe not, but it supports my theory that you were once involved with Mia. Be honest, did she send you those flowers?"

"You tell me. She's your girlfriend. Does it seem like something Mia would do?"

Lillian's shoulders sagged. "No, it doesn't. But she's been acting so strange. I thought maybe..."

Camille looked Lillian directly in the eye. "The flowers are from someone else."

"But you were involved with her."

"Why can't you let this go?"

"Why can't you tell me the truth?"

"Because it's personal."

"Don't you think it's personal to me too?"

Camille sighed in defeat. "Would you like a drink?" If she was going to talk about Mia, alcohol was in order. A nice single malt, or scotch-guard as she liked to think of it.

"Fuck yes."

The expletive fell so easily out of Lillian's mouth Camille wondered if this would be her first drink of the evening.

"Scotch?"

"Absolutely."

"Single malt?"

"Perfect. I take it neat."

Camille shook her head. Of course she did. Mia also preferred her single malt straight up. Camille had not learned until a few years ago that adding a few drops of water actually opened the flavor, instead of diluting it as Mia had always insisted. She pulled the bottle of eighteen-year-old Macallan from the liquor cabinet and placed it on the table in front of them next to two cut-crystal glasses. It was the brand Mia had introduced her to, the only vestige of their time together that Camille had not cast aside.

Lillian snorted when she saw the bottle. "This just keeps getting better."

"Do you want a drink or not?"

"Please."

Camille unscrewed the lid and poured three fingers neat into Lillian's glass. She gave herself an equal measure, splashed in some water and then returned to the table. Taking a seat across from Lillian, she raised her drink in toast.

"To comfortable shoes."

Lillian clinked her glass against Camille's. "I'll drink to that." They both savored the Macallan. Camille imagined she knew the questions Lillian wanted to ask. She knew the things she would have asked had she been given the opportunity eight years ago. She took a large sip and plunged right in.

"I hated wearing them too," Camille commiserated, "but she said they made my legs look pretty."

Lillian took another pull of her scotch. "That's what she says to me."

"Well, for the record, she's not wrong." Camille smiled at Lillian who rolled her eyes. "But do you like wearing them?"

"I like pleasing Mia, so…" Lillian's voice trailed off, as if she were only considering for the first time how this might sound.

Camille nodded. "I can relate. She has a way of making you feel her whims are more important than your own needs. I once missed my cousin's baby shower because Mia needed me to wait for the cable guy."

Lillian blinked away fresh tears. "It's so confusing. I don't feel taken advantage of. I'm not the kind of person who chases around after people, you know." She leveled her gaze at Camille. "I do things for Mia because I want to do them. Because…" she searched for an explanation.

"Because, you're in love with her?"

"Probably."

"It's not a crime."

"At the law firm it is."

"Believe me, I'm aware of Walker and Jenkins' no-fraternization rule." Camille thought of Hannah's plan to cook her dinner tomorrow night, followed by Hannah's perfect body for dessert. No matter how many Gowear cases Mia threw at her, Camille didn't want to give her up.

"Were you in love with her?"

"Who? Mia?"

"Who else?"

"Yes," Camille said, leveling with her. "I was. Or at least I thought I was. I was very young. It was a long time ago."

"Was she in love with you?" Lillian's voice was small.

"I wanted to believe that she was. But looking back, I don't think so. She certainly never said the words."

"So, you're not sure?"

"Why do you want to know? Why is that piece of it important?"

"Because I need to know if she's capable of giving her heart to someone. And if the answer is yes, I want that someone to be me."

"Oh." This was not what Camille had expected to hear. "Well, that's easy. The answer is no. She never gave her heart to me."

"Oh." Lillian seemed disappointed. "Will you tell me about your relationship. It might help me to understand her. You know? I'm just so confused."

Camille hesitated. The memories she'd hoped to relive tonight were not those of her time spent with Mia. Jenna was still waiting for the download and was probably livid that Camille hadn't called her back. She took a sip of her scotch. "It always felt like she was perfectly comfortable with our relationship being secret. Like she was almost happy there was a no-frat rule at work."

"Yes!"

"But there was real intimacy too. She wasn't a lost cause. Maybe that's why it took me two years to give up on her."

"Why did you?"

"My mom died. It made me reevaluate a lot of things."

"I'm sorry."

"Thank you. As I said, it was a long time ago." Camille noticed that Lillian's glass was empty. She picked up the Macallan and poured her another finger, and then added one to her own glass. She sipped her drink. Countless hours of therapy had distilled her opinion of Mia down to its essence. No matter how successful the woman was professionally, no matter how many cases she won or clients she landed, Mia was an emotional coward. Not a monster, but a chicken. Her need to be the dominant partner in the relationship only underlined this fact. Camille raised the glass to the light and considered how she might best express this opinion to Lillian without offending her.

"Just don't let her bully you."

Lillian giggled. The Macallan, added to whatever she'd consumed earlier, was having an impact. "I actually don't mind that part so much, and she only thinks she's in control, anyway."

"Oh, okay. Good for you." Camille tapped Lillian's glass with her own and the younger woman smiled.

"Yes, well, it's not good for me if she's trying to fuck you again."

"That's not going to happen."

"How can you resist?" Drunk Lillian was indignant. "Mia is smart, sophisticated, and beautiful!"

Camille was bemused. "I thought you wanted me to stay away from her."

"I do!"

"There's nothing to worry about. Believe me."

"What about New York?"

"I'm not going to New York. Mia can't make me do anything I don't want to do. I'll be very clear with her. If she won't listen to me, she'll listen to Human Resources."

Lillian looked alarmed. "That could affect her career!"

"Like it's not affecting mine? But don't worry. It won't come to that. I'll draft a complaint and she'll back down, I promise."

"How do you know?"

"I know," Camille said, "because it worked last time."

CHAPTER FOURTEEN

Mia Culpa

When Camille arrived at Walker and Jenkins the next day, Jenna was waiting in Beverly Stanley's office FaceTiming Melissa on her laptop. Camille had postponed the debrief with Jenna the night before pleading exhaustion. Being denied the information dump for an additional twelve hours had not made Jenna happy, but she'd settled when Camille had promised full disclosure along with cinnamon rolls. She closed the office door.

The two women looked at her like kids expecting a story around a campfire. Camille didn't disappoint. Launching into the saga, she began from when she and Hannah left Molly's Diner and spared no detail. She even described the make out session in the tearoom. When Jenna's already largish eyes popped into caricature, Camille wondered if she'd shared too much. Melissa's features had adopted a benign countenance that Camille imagined she reserved for patients who were about to be told bad news. Scandalized or not, it didn't stop them from asking questions.

"I can't believe you felt up a local celebrity in a manky tearoom!"

"The place was completely empty," Camille defended herself. "And Hannah's not exactly a celebrity."

Jenna tapped a sleek black folder, conspicuous on the desk in front of her. "Hannah Richards is a serious player, Camille. You won't believe what I found last night." She pushed the folder toward Camille, as Melissa spoke up through the monitor.

"I thought you weren't going to bring that thing to the office. I thought you were going to wait until Camille said she wanted to see it."

"She wants to see it."

"What is it?" Camille picked up the folder and saw the first section was filled with printouts of newspaper and magazine articles. Hannah was the subject of every one.

"Where did you get this?"

"Just look at it," Jenna directed. "It's a dossier on the woman you felt up in the manky tearoom."

"The tearoom wasn't manky! And, oh my, wow."

Camille's eyes sparked at an image of Hannah cliff-diving in some unnamed tropical paradise. It was another Gowear cover and Hannah's nipples were visible through the fabric of her suit. Camille sucked in a breath. The caption beneath the photo read *Dare to Soar.* She turned the pages to a photo of Hannah and her friend Bree standing in front of their climbing gym. As usual, Hannah was wearing a tight black bodysuit and the flirty grin that made Camille's heart flip. Jenna had been very thorough. There were photos of Hannah cutting the ribbon at an LGBTQ community center. There was even a piece from her college newspaper. Entitled *Goal Averse*, it profiled Hannah's standout role as goalie for Stanford's women's soccer team. There were dozens more pages that Camille wanted to devour like a newly discovered Harry Potter novel, but she managed to restrain herself. She would look at it later, in private.

Turning to the second section of the folder she noticed the printouts looked more official. Incredulous, she thumbed through what appeared to be Gowear's financial statements, tax returns, and even a PowerPoint showing sales projections for the next five years. "Where did you get all this?"

"It was a basic Google search." Jenna acted as if the information was nothing, but Melissa yelled from the screen.

"That's not true! She was up all night, scrapbooking that woman's life."

Jenna glared at her wife but then relented. "Okay, it was an advanced Google search," she admitted. "And maybe I was showing off a little bit. But your girl is really something. Not only is she super rich," Jenna tapped the folder, "but she's a philanthropist, a model, and a badass athlete."

"She's not my girl."

"Well, she was yesterday."

Camille thought of Hannah's face. Her look of sweet abandon when Camille had touched her intimately in the foyer of the Dupont Circle townhouse. "And maybe tonight," she said, causing Melissa to hoot.

"Maybe? What does that mean?"

"She's cooking me dinner."

"That's not a maybe!" Melissa and Jenna said simultaneously, and then laughed with delight.

"You're probably right," Camille acknowledged, blushing. It felt good sharing confidences with her old friends.

"How was the sex?" Jenna wanted to know.

"Jenna!" Melissa chided her wife.

"You want the answer just as much as I do!"

"Yes, but you can't ask her like that."

"I just did."

Camille cut off the debate. "The sex was amazing."

"Oh, I'm so glad," Melissa said.

"Tell us everything!"

"Jenna!"

"It was so good that I'm going back tonight. Client or no client, I'm taking the risk."

"Well, okay." Jenna clapped her hands together.

"No arguing with that," Melissa agreed. "Just be careful."

"You don't know the half of it."

Camille filled them in on Lillian's unexpected visit.

"Throwback Thursday came to your house at night?" Jenna was astonished.

"She did."

"That's crazy."

"And completely unprofessional," Melissa added.

"I know. I tried to keep it impersonal but she started crying."

"So you decided to invite her in and ply her with two hundred and fifty-dollar scotch?"

"Pretty much." Camille turned to Melissa. "It was strictly medicinal."

"Oh, I'm sure."

"And now, apparently, we're besties."

"What? No!" Jenna was having none of it. "I'm your bestie. We've just found each other again. Lillian is way too young for you."

"I'm only kidding. But it did get personal. We talked about Mia, sort of compared notes."

"No way!" Jenna picked up a Washington Nationals fidget spinner from Beverly Stanley's desk. Pinching it between her thumb and forefinger, she twirled it until it became a red blur. "Does Mia make Lillian shave her pussy bald too?"

"Honey!" Melissa shouted through the monitor but Camille took it in stride.

"We actually didn't get that far. She was mostly concerned that I might be sleeping with her girlfriend."

"She asked you that?"

Camille nodded. "She thinks Mia is making a play for me to avoid what's happening with them."

"What's happening with them?"

"It's the same old story. Mia's scared of commitment."

"What's that got to do with you?"

"I'm the distraction."

"That's an interesting theory," Melissa mused. "What's your read on it?"

"I can totally see it. I broke up with her after my mom died. I was tired of keeping the relationship a secret and told her so. But it really hurt when she let me go. Before that, I believed she was the one."

"And now?" Melissa asked softly.

"I feel nothing for her at all."

"Really? Nothing?" Jenna challenged.

"Okay," Camille acknowledged. "I'm angry that she's dragged me into her drama."

"I can understand that," Melissa agreed.

"What does Lillian want you to do?" Jenna wanted to know.

"She wants me to make it clear to Mia that I'm not interested in sleeping with her, which I'm not. But it's tricky with the partnership tied up in it. She could still blackball me."

Jenna spun the fidget spinner again. "This is so fucked up."

"Have you thought of bringing Human Resources into it?" Melissa asked.

Camille picked up a piece of paper from the desk. "I've drafted a letter of complaint, but it's just a bluff. I won't file it."

"Why not?"

"I'm involved with a client, remember?"

"Yeah, but is the relationship serious enough to risk the partnership?" Jenna put down the toy and picked up the black folder. She flipped through the pages of photos of Hannah on the arm of various beautiful women. When she got to the cover of the Gowear catalog, Camille stilled her hand. Her eyes caressed Hannah's nearly perfect physique. She let them linger on the floating lotus tattoo. She remembered biting the supple skin just above her shoulder.

"It might be."

"The sex is that good?"

"It is." Camille blushed. "But I also really like her. It makes me happy to be with her."

"Well I guess so, if you felt her up in a manky tearoom."

"It wasn't manky!"

"Melissa?"

"That tearoom is manky as hell, Camille. Good luck with Mia. I've got to go do rounds. Love you baby, see you at home."

"Love you." Melissa disappeared from the screen and Jenna closed the laptop. She turned to Camille with a sigh.

"It's tricky stuff, Cam-o-flage."

"And by tricky, you mean painful?"

"Exactly."

"I can't believe that Mia is trying to manipulate me into staying in DC."

Jenna snorted. "You can't? That woman ran you around town like you were her show dog. She gets off on being in charge. Pushing people around is her signature style."

Camille shook her head. "I loathe her signature style."

"Her signature style sucks." Jenna stood and smoothed the fabric of her dress over the ample curves of her hips. "When are you going to talk to her?"

"Now, actually. I've scheduled a meeting with her this morning." Camille put the black folder on top of a stack of Washington Nationals books and picked up the HR letter. She slipped it into a file folder. "I'll walk you out."

"You're going there now? On an empty stomach?"

Camille gave Jenna the bag of cinnamon rolls they'd forgotten to eat. "I'll be fine."

"Do you want me to come with you?"

"Under what pretense?"

Jenna stopped short. She was no longer joking. "As your friend? Mia is out of line, Camille. I saw how she treated you eight years ago. We can't let her do it again. I'll talk to HR myself." Her luminous eyes shone with righteous indignation causing Camille to smile. She pulled Jenna into an impromptu hug.

"Thank you for saying we," Camille said into her ear, and released her.

"Of course." Jenna wasn't giving up. "I'm serious. Do you want me to come with you?"

"No, but I appreciate that you offered, I really do."

Jenna only let Camille go after she'd agreed to a follow-up debrief the next evening over cocktails. Melissa was working a night shift and Jenna wanted to stay in the city for a drink. She'd even offered to pay for the first round. Camille had readily agreed. A showdown with Mia and the date with Hannah would be too much to process alone. She was thankful to have a friend like Jenna who, aside from demanding baked goods, had no agenda beyond Camille's happiness.

Mia's office faced the rear courtyard of the building where patio seating served the building's ground-level food court. Mia preferred being far away from reception and the main entrance. A private, guarded woman, her success hadn't come through her people skills. Johnny Jenkins, the deceased founding partner of the law firm, had fondly called his young protégeé The Viper. Deadly and beautiful, watchful and waiting, she lulled you into a sense of calm and then moved in for the kill. Once upon a time, Camille had found this attribute sexy. She'd been proud of her lover's ability to annihilate the competition with a single, scathing comment. Even when on the receiving end, Camille couldn't help but admire the precision strike of the blow.

Mia's office was spacious and lovely. It had an en suite bathroom that Camille remembered very well. The amenity had played a starring role in their affair. Often when working late, Mia would lure Camille into the small room, pin her against the nineteenth-century tile floor and fuck her until she screamed into the lavender throw rug. Afterward, she'd rinse her hands in the sink with a special citrus soap, like she'd been chopping onions. Camille would fix her skirt and they'd return to work.

Camille blanched at the memory. What had once seemed incredibly hot now felt dirty, contaminated. The first glimpse of Lillian had shattered any remaining illusions that her own connection with Mia had been special. Though Camille had longed for something more meaningful, she now knew the affair had been nothing more than a convenience. The memory was painful enough, but Mia's current behavior was shocking. Using Camille as a smokescreen to avoid her feelings for Lillian was galling. How dare she? Not only was it unprofessional, it was thoughtless and cruel. If Camille still had feelings for Mia, the result might have been devastating.

Suddenly the door was in front of her. Years ago they'd had a code, two short raps followed by one loud knock. Today, she didn't bother. Twisting the handle, Camille entered the room unannounced.

She heard Mia before she saw her. A soft keening sound was coming from the area behind the cherrywood desk. Camille's first thought was that a robotic vacuum cleaner had been trapped beneath the chair. Then she saw a foot. She crossed the room, and the foot grew into an ankle, and the ankle grew into a leg.

"Mia?" The word hung suspended in the air. To Camille it sounded like an accusation. "Is this a bad time?"

The keening stopped, and there was a collection of small sniffs.

"Are you okay?" Camille ventured again. "I can come back."

"What do you want?" A voice, small and hollow, came from the space beneath the cherry desk.

"We had a meeting. But it looks like it's a bad time. We can reschedule."

"She broke up with me."

"She what?" Against her better judgment, Camille moved toward the desk.

"Lillian."

Camille listened aghast as Mia hiccupped herself into another fit of tears. In the two years they'd been together, Camille had never seen Mia cry. Her go-to emotion had been a steely anger, which inspired more fear than sympathy. Vulnerable Mia was new. Despite Camille's bitter feelings, she had to empathize. Nothing hurt more than having your heart broken.

"Oh, Mia." Camille rolled the office chair out of the way and crouched low by the desk to see her former lover. Their eyes met under the desk. "What are you doing?"

"Messing things up. Just like usual."

Camille held her gaze. Normally inscrutable, Mia's face was an open book of pain. Camille was stunned to see an expression of naked regret that seemed to encompass more than just the situation with Lillian. In it, she imagined she saw the ghosts of other loves lost and possibly even an apology. The Viper had been struck.

"What happened?"

"I blew it."

Camille extended her hand. Though Mia appeared quite comfortable, curled in a fetal position beneath the desk, the crouch was not working for Camille.

"Let me help you up."

Mia huffed out a breath. "Take a seat. I'll be up in a minute."

"No." It was understandable that Mia wanted a minute to collect herself, but the vulnerable state suited Camille much better. "Give me your hand."

Relenting, Mia stretched out a hand to grasp Camille's. There was no feeling of recognition. Mia's palm was moist and clammy. It felt like a limp rag. Camille pulled her from the hide-a-way and directed her into the large leather office chair. Throne like, it had been selected to elevate the diminutive Mia above her visitors. Atop its hand-stitched elegance Camille watched her inflate.

"What do you want, Camille?"

"Lillian came to see me last night. She told me she was in love with you."

At the mention of the younger woman's name, fresh tears spilled from Mia's eyes. She shook her head. "Why would she do that?"

"Because, as usual, you're behaving like an emotional coward. Jeopardizing everything because you can't be honest about your feelings. Does that sound about right?"

"I can't be in a relationship with Lillian. It's against the firm's policy. You know better than anyone."

"I know it's been a convenient excuse."

"The partners would never allow it."

"Then move to another firm."

"Excuse me?"

Camille waved her hands around the tastefully decorated office. "Find a new job. Leave this place. Partners move to new firms all the time."

Mia looked as if she'd been struck. "That's absurd. I couldn't possibly leave, not after everything I've built here."

"Then see if Lillian would be willing to take a new job. Surely you could help her find something? Then you two could properly date. Everyone wins."

A glimmer of hope flickered in the inky black eyes. "Do you think she would?"

Camille wanted to punch her. How could someone so confident in their professional life be such an emotional sissy? "There's no way to know unless you ask her."

"Would you have done it?"

Though Camille knew exactly what Mia was asking, she wanted to hear her say the words. "Would I have done what?"

"Would you have left the firm, if I'd asked you to?"

Camille rose from the chair. Turning, she picked up the file with the HR complaint letter inside. "Well, you never asked me, so we'll never know." She put the file down on the desk in front of Mia. "I'm not going with you to New York. I've drafted an email to HR outlining a harassment claim against you. I'm assuming it's no longer necessary."

Mia eyed the file but did not touch it. "That's correct."

"Great. I'd prefer to go back to California in peace, not pieces."

"I completely understand."

Camille gave her a hard look. "I expect to have the Fabray settlement signed very soon." She said a silent prayer to Cory. "But then I'm off Gowear. No wetsuit. No smokescreen."

"Agreed."

"Thank you. Good luck with Lillian."

Mia gave a rare self-deprecating smile. "I don't deserve her."

"No, you don't." Camille turned and left the room.

CHAPTER FIFTEEN

Petrichor

It was at least a mile and a half from Joe Robbins's house to Hannah's brownstone, but Camille felt like walking. She felt like skipping actually. Her current state of happiness was far too inflated to stuff into an Uber, so she set out on foot. The day had been momentous, a game changer. If Camille kept a journal, the page would warrant a starred entry. She still couldn't believe it. The indomitable Mia had shown a crack in her armor and it was right above her heart. Camille couldn't have been more surprised if someone had told her that bacon was a vegetable, harvested from a bush in southern New Zealand.

When Camille had prepared for the meeting, she'd envisioned many scenarios. Coaxing a sobbing woman from beneath her desk hadn't been one of them. She'd found herself ad libbing, channeling her mother's voice and manner. Though dogged in her activism, Mary Robbins had been the model of restraint. She'd liked to say that you attracted more flies with honey and went to jail far less often. Mia had rolled over like a family dog on the welcome mat.

The victory was bittersweet. True to form, Mia had been too wrapped up in her own agenda to notice the impropriety of the shoulder she'd chosen to lean on. Camille chafed at the confession. Though she applauded the progress in Mia's emotional journey, it stung to have been used as a way station.

On some level, it would always hurt but now Camille felt lighter, free. It was as if she'd removed a heavy coat she hadn't known she'd been wearing. Knowledge that Lulu Fabray had signed the settlement papers had lightened her mood even more. Not only had Cory made contact with the reclusive model, he'd talked her into leaving the ashram and coming with him to the spa in Flagstaff. It seemed incredible. But, according to his text, they'd stopped by Starbucks for a quick latte, before FedExing the papers to Camille on the way out of town. She could now fraternize with Hannah until the cows came home. And this was now the issue before her. Three thousand miles was a long way for cows to travel. Was there even a point?

Camille thought of the black folder she'd left in Beverly Stanley's office. Jenna's in-depth research indicated Hannah Richards was an outright player. It would be silly to begin thinking of what they shared in relationship terms. Camille needed to see it for what it was. Hannah was a bolt of sunshine in her life, radiant but temporary. She resolved to soak up every drop.

Crossing out of Woodley Park, she crossed the Duke Ellington Bridge into Adams Morgan. She'd misjudged the weather. A cloud bank was directly in front of her, hovering like a heavy blanket. It was definitely going to rain, but when? She considered calling an Uber but the walk felt great and she was more than halfway to Hannah's. There was a good chance she'd make it before the storm broke.

Camille took a deep breath and inhaled the smell that often came before the rain, a distinct odor called petrichor. It was the smell of plant oils being released into the air after a long dry period and a wholly appropriate scent for her day. Yesterday had set a new standard. What she'd experienced with Hannah had woken her to a potential she didn't know existed. Possibly it was a fluke, a one-off reaction to pent-up energy. Today, she would find out.

She was nearly there when the sky opened up, but she made no move to hasten her pace. Camille couldn't remember the last time she'd walked in the rain. It was glorious and she welcomed the downpour as if it were a cleansing shower. Everything felt new and possible. She imagined the rain was washing the last vestiges of Mia from her body into the street where they drained into the gutter, into the Potomac, and eventually out to sea.

By the time Camille stepped under the protective overhang of Hannah's porch, she was soaked through to her skin. She caught a glimpse of her reflection in the storm door and gasped. The light cotton sundress she'd carefully chosen for the warm spring day was plastered against her body like a napkin on a cocktail glass, the lace of her matching pale pink bra and panties clearly visible beneath. She pulled the wet dress away from her skin but at best she looked like she was wearing a bikini under a sodden cover-up. Why hadn't she called an Uber?

Suddenly the big wooden door opened, and Hannah was there, filling the entrance with the warmth of her smile. The golden eyes danced with delight at the sight of Camille's state of dishabille.

"Oh, hello." She reached out her hand, and softly stroked Camille's face with the tips of her fingers. "I love your outfit."

"Hi," Camille managed to say. Under the intensity of Hannah's gaze, her nipples sprang to attention. They, at least, were not the least bit conflicted regarding their feelings for the woman in front of her. If only everything were that simple. Camille leaned her cheek into the caress.

"Come here, sexy." Hannah pulled Camille easily over the threshold and into her arms. Their bodies came together, and Camille heard herself moan with pleasure. Seriously, what was the matter with her? They'd been apart barely twenty-four hours and Camille was reacting as if it had been weeks. She captured Hannah's mouth in a hungry kiss. What she couldn't explain in words she'd try to convey with her lips. To occupy her hands she wove them into Hannah's hair, pushing them into the rich, red strands. She wanted to avoid taking liberties with the beautiful body, at least until after dinner.

Hannah pushed the front door closed with her foot and Camille's backpack fell to the floor. The wine bottle inside clanked against the hardwood of the entrance hall. When Camille looked down to make sure it hadn't broken, she noticed Hannah's black silk shirt was wet. Horrified, she tried to step back from the embrace to get a better look.

"I'm getting you all wet!"

Hannah only held on more tightly. Her eyes were warm, and full of fun. Slowly, she walked Camille back against the wall of the entrance hall and pressed a thigh between her legs. "You have no idea."

The pressure against Camille's center felt delicious, but the contact wasn't doing Hannah's expensive-looking blouse any favors. She made one last attempt. "But your shirt."

"Shhhhhh." Hannah silenced her with a kiss that caused Camille to forget about anything fabric oriented. Her entire focus became the hot, wet tongue that had slipped inside her mouth, and was lazily stroking her own. She ground her hips into the hard muscle of Hannah's thigh. Spreading her legs a little wider, she felt her head began to swim.

"Should we go upstairs?"

Hannah gave her a playful look. "If you want. But I kind of thought foyer fucking was our thing."

Camille blushed at the memory of her eagerness the day before. She leaned her forehead against Hannah's. "Foyer fucking isn't a thing."

"It's not?" Hannah slid her hand beneath the hem of Camille's dress. She moved her long fingers up Camille's leg, resting them just shy of Camille's equally damp underwear.

"No, it's not." Camille licked her lips as Hannah pushed her panties aside and began to tease her slit. She slid a finger half inside Camille's already soaking center. "Are you sure? Because I've been thinking about it all day."

"I guess it could be." Camille swallowed hard. She lifted a knee to allow Hannah better access. The redhead pushed her finger in more deeply. Ever so gently, she began to pulse her hand, stoking Camille's need for more. The entire time Hannah kept her eyes locked on Camille's. As usual, they were dancing.

"Are you starting to remember?" She increased the rhythm of her stroke and laughed when Camille's hips thrust forward seeking more pressure.

"I am." Camille shamelessly rocked her pelvis against Hannah's hand. There was no point in being coy when someone was fucking you against a wall.

"I thought you might," Hannah whispered in her ear and then gave Camille what she was asking for. On her next thrust she pushed the heel of her palm hard into Camille's swollen center.

"Oh God, that's good." Camille opened her stance wider and pressed herself into Hannah's hand. She responded by dipping her head and biting Camille's nipple through the fabric of her dress and bra.

"Take this off," she said, her voice no longer playful.

Camille moved to unbutton the dress as Hannah kept working her fingers. With every thrust, she tapped Camille's clit with her palm, driving her passion higher. Somehow Camille managed to free her shoulders from the sodden dress and unfasten her bra. Hannah immediately claimed a nipple tightly between her teeth. The pleasure was so intense Camille cried out. Pushing her shoulders back, she laid her head against the wall, her mouth falling helplessly open as Hannah continued to claim her.

The pressure built until she couldn't take it any longer. Camille exploded into Hannah's hand and again, it was the redhead's name on her lips as she cried out her release.

"Hannah, Hannah, Hannah," she gasped, rocking her hips as the spasms shot through her body. The inside walls of her core contracted against Hannah's fingers, pulling them more deeply inside her.

"I've got you." Hannah held her carefully in place. She bit Camille's neck. "You are so sexy."

She stopped working her fingers but made no move to extract them from Camille's heat. As residual spasms shook Camille's body, Hannah began to kiss her again. When their lips fused together once more, Camille whimpered. For something that was meant to be casual she was feeling way too many emotions. Camille's body reacted to Hannah's on a primal level. There was no other way to explain it. Camille had never experienced anything so powerful and determined it must be Hannah's skill as a lover. All thought was pushed from her mind when Hannah began pulsing her fingers again.

"God, Hannah," Camille moaned softly at the first stroke causing Hannah to still her hand and break their kiss.

She looked sweetly into Camille's eyes. "Are you ready for more?" She slid a single finger deeper inside Camille, testing her.

Camille bucked her hips in reply, and sucked Hannah's tongue greedily back into her mouth. Their kisses grew sloppy as Camille climbed toward a second orgasm. Hannah licked a swipe up Camille's neck, and then began sucking the sensitive spot just beneath Camille's ear.

"I love foyer fucking," she whispered, and pushed the heel of her hand into Camille's clit. That was all it took. The orgasm was so powerful that Camille didn't make any noise at all this time. Later she was surprised she hadn't passed out. Hannah had taken her to a whole new level. It was incredible, beyond the beyond.

When Hannah finally slid her hand free, they were both breathing hard. Mirroring Camille's action from the previous day, Hannah brought her fingers to her lips and licked them clean. Camille let her leg drop to the floor and straightened her dress. When she looked up, Hannah was smiling at her happily, her eyes alight with success. Camille smiled back. "Pleased with yourself?"

"I'm pleased with you," Hannah replied and captured Camille's mouth in another languorous kiss. Camille could taste herself on Hannah's lips and moaned at the intimacy of the sensation. They continued kissing for several minutes and may have erupted into another full-blown episode had a buzzer not sounded in the kitchen.

Hannah pulled back. "Eggplant parmesan."

"You made eggplant parmesan?"

"Is that okay?"

"It's great. It's actually my favorite."

"That's good news." Hannah leaned over to retrieve the backpack from the floor and Camille saw her black silk shirt had come untucked from the fitted jeans. The front was now a complete mess.

"Oh my God, your shirt!"

Hannah looked down at her rumpled outfit, and grinned. "Totally worth it." She gave Camille another kiss and directed her toward the kitchen. As they walked through the central hallway, Camille peered into rooms she'd only glimpsed the day before. Hannah's taste was sophisticated without being pretentious. Camille saw evidence of careful thought everywhere. It was a reminder of her own sad lack of furnishings. She began to fantasize about strolling through antique stores with Hannah, and then stopped herself. Hannah was not a permanent fixture in her life. She lived on the other side of the country and dated lots of beautiful women. There was little chance she'd help Camille pick out a living room set. Camille needed to calm down.

As they neared the kitchen, the alarm grew louder. Camille could see a light blinking on top of the stove. Hannah let go of her hand and picked up an oven mitt, Camille looked around the kitchen appreciatively. The back wall was entirely glass and looked out onto a garden patio. In the dwindling light, Camille saw a koi pond and an herb garden. More evidence of thought and care. The kitchen bordered on grand. State-of-the-art appliances were seamlessly blended into the early twentieth-century decor. Camille was just starting to consider appliances for her townhouse and knew she was looking at over a hundred thousand dollars' worth of equipment. The Miele refrigerator alone cost at least ten grand. An espresso machine looked as if it might have come from the Ritz in Rome.

"Wow," Camille said.

"What?"

Hannah opened the door of a dual-range Viking stove, the envy of any caterer, and pulled out a tray of golden fried eggplant baking in a bed of marinara and parmesan. Flecks of basil dotted the pan and Camille inhaled deeply as Hannah placed it on a trivet.

"Your kitchen is really fancy."

Hannah snorted. "It's embarrassing."

The answer surprised Camille. "Why is it embarrassing to have a beautiful kitchen? You obviously cook."

Hannah rolled her eyes. "Stacey, the shopping step-monster, picked out all the appliances."

"Oh." Camille bit her tongue. Just because the conflict of interest had been resolved did not make it okay to discuss the case.

Hannah checked a large pot of water on the stove. It had just begun to boil so she added a package of fresh pasta from the refrigerator.

"The kitchen was Stacey's housewarming gift to me. She insisted. There was a connection through a decorator or something. I didn't pay attention until it was too late."

"Well I'd kill for the stove and fridge." Camille changed the subject. "But I might need a barista class to work your coffeemaker."

"I'd be happy to teach you." Hannah gave Camille a sweet smile.

Camille smiled back but then shivered involuntarily and hugged herself. Though her clothing was back in place, she was still drenched from the rain, and beginning to feel uncomfortably chilled.

Hannah was quick to notice.

"You're cold."

The genuine tone of concern made Camille's heart swell.

"Why don't you go take a shower and I'll finish making dinner? You can put on my robe when you get out. It's hanging on the bathroom door."

The plan was too sensible to argue. "Thank you." Camille pressed her lips softly against Hannah's.

She made a small noise in the back of her throat. "You do remember where my bedroom is? Because I'd be happy to show you." Her eyes were full of invitation.

Camille reached out and stroked her cheek. "Just so we're clear, there's nothing I don't remember about your bedroom. Nothing. And I'm happy to revisit the details, anytime you like." Hannah bit her lip, and the golden eyes narrowed.

"But?"

They studied each other, as the pendulum swung between the thoughtfully prepared meal and another session of urgent coupling. Camille looked hesitantly at the tray of eggplant parmesan, and the momentum swung toward the food. She couldn't allow her libido to preempt Hannah's time and effort.

"You put too much work into this meal."

"Are you sure?" Hannah made a move to switch off the boiling water. "We can heat this up later."

"I know." Camille laid her hand boldly against Hannah's sex. "But we can heat this up too."

CHAPTER SIXTEEN

Laying it all on the Table

Hannah's bathrobe smelled of Johnson's baby shampoo. Camille had previously detected the scent in the glorious red hair but hadn't been able identify it until she saw the iconic bottle in Hannah's shower. No more tears. Camille prayed it was a prophecy. The brand certainly fit the woman. Though in her mid-thirties, Hannah radiated the vitality of a person half her age. It wasn't just her exquisite body, though that was certainly a contributing factor, but a *joie de vivre* that crackled around her like an energy field.

It was a welcome contrast to most of the women Camille knew. Admittedly, most of the women Camille knew were lawyers at her firm. Colleagues, not friends. Other than recreational sex with Val and her intensive therapy sessions, her personal intimacies did not extend beyond Cory and she mostly only saw him at work. Camille hadn't even befriended the woman who cut her hair. She told herself that her job precluded a personal life. How could she be the best if she didn't put in the extra time?

Being with Hannah felt like turning her face into the sun. There was an air of spontaneity about her that suggested anything might happen, a look in her eye that let you know she wasn't taking things too seriously. The look not only urged Camille to follow Hannah's lead, but somehow gave her permission to do so. There also was the fact that Hannah rode a purple motorcycle. It was almost too much sexy for one woman to bear.

Camille pressed her nose into the spongy softness of the bathrobe. Securing the belt, she groaned. How was she going to resist falling in love with her? Already she could feel her heart slipping. Hannah had never had a girlfriend and lived three thousand miles away. The entire situation was preposterous.

The oversized bathrobe enveloped her like a hug. Camille imagined it draped over Hannah's naked body and shivered as her clit pulsed to attention. She was still aroused from the foyer fucking and looking forward to taking her turn with Hannah after dinner. The woman's body was a masterpiece. Camille still couldn't believe she was allowed to touch it. The thing belonged behind a velvet rope.

She went downstairs and found Hannah setting the kitchen table. Camille paused in the doorway to watch her fold a cloth napkin into an elaborate swan. Familiar music was playing from a wireless speaker. It was soft jazz with a female vocalist. After a few bars Camille realized it was "I Left My Heart in San Francisco," and smiled at the coincidence. How long before she would be back on the other side of the country? It was the last thing she wanted to think about tonight.

Camille surveyed the carefully laid table and was surprised to feel emotional. It had been a long time since someone had taken this much care for her. Maybe since her mother had died. She pushed back the tears. The food had already been plated and was sitting on the counter waiting to be served. Camille's wine rested in a beautiful stoneware cooler between two stemless glasses. An elaborate Victorian candelabra was alight next to a delicate bouquet of flowers in varying shades of pink. Like Hannah, it was simply gorgeous.

"The table is beautiful."

"Thank you."

The music changed and Camille heard the first notes of The Eagles' "Hotel California."

"I love this song."

"Me too."

A thought struck her. "It's another California song."

Hannah blushed. "Is it?"

"It definitely is." Camille cocked an eyebrow and Hannah's blush deepened.

"I may have made a playlist."

"You made a playlist?" Camille was delighted. "What else is on it?"

"Wait and see."

They smiled at each other and Camille saw that the fire they'd lit earlier in the foyer was still smoldering in the golden gaze. Hannah made no attempt to hide her desire, allowing her eyes to sweep Camille's body with obvious appreciation. At the boldness of Hannah's stare, Camille's clit began to throb again, heightening her awareness that she was wearing nothing beneath the borrowed clothing.

"My robe looks good on you."

"Thank you. I love the fabric." Camille burrowed deeply into the bathrobe to hide the blush creeping up her neck. "What's it made of?"

"Bamboo," Hannah replied matter-of-factly. She picked up the plates from the counter and transferred them to the table. "Oprah has one just like it."

Camille laughed. "Oprah! How do you know that?"

"Jane's mother, Ruth, ordered it from the QVC Channel. According to Jane, she has them on speed dial. They gave it to me for my birthday."

"When was your birthday?"

"Last week. We went to Lake Tahoe to celebrate. It's kind of a tradition. That's why you didn't see me on the escalator." Hannah pulled a chair out from the table and gestured for Camille to sit down. "Milady?"

As always, a smile played around her beautiful mouth. Touched by Hannah's gesture, Camille found she was unable to resist kissing her. So she didn't. When their lips met, Hannah slid an arm around Camille's waist and pulled her close against her body. They both moaned, and the kiss ratcheted from zero to sixty in an instant. Camille allowed herself to revel in the marvelous sensations conjured up by Hannah's talented tongue but when the song changed to "California Dreaming" by the Mamas and the Papas, she took the opportunity to pull away. Too much effort had gone into the dinner. They could certainly control themselves for the half hour it would take to enjoy the meal. They were both adults after all. Camille met Hannah's lust-filled gaze, and remembered she was two orgasms ahead of her. Okay, fifteen minutes would be ample time to eat.

"Another great song," she said as Hannah released her into the chair and took the one across from her.

"Thank you." Hannah took a sip of wine.

Camille did the same and found the cool liquid refreshing against her kiss-stung lips. She set her glass down on the table. "How long has Lake Tahoe been a birthday tradition?"

"About fifteen years. We started going out there in college. One of the girls on the team had a house. We just Airbnb now." Camille was given the impression that Hannah wanted to say something else but was holding back.

"Who goes besides you and Bree?"

"Other women from our college soccer team. Most of them are married now. Some even have kids."

"Do they bring their families?"

"Sometimes. I..." Hannah started a thought but didn't continue.

This time, when she reached for her wine, Camille caught her hand.

"What were you going to say?"

"Nothing." Hannah blushed adorably and looked down at her plate.

Camille tightened her grip. "If it's nothing, then you shouldn't have a problem telling me." She circled her thumb over the number one tattooed on Hannah's wrist. When she reached her pulse point, she pressed down, causing Hannah to look up and meet her eye. In their golden depths, Camille was surprised to see uncertainty. When Hannah finally spoke, her voice was measured.

"I was going to say, that we've been going to Lake Tahoe for many years and it's always been a great time." She blinked her eyes but didn't look away. "But this year wasn't as much fun because I was distracted by a woman I'd just met. A woman who wasn't there but is here now."

"Oh," Camille said and broke into a goofy grin that threatened to split her face in two. Her heart flooded with adrenaline. *Hannah had missed her.* They smiled sweetly at each other for a long minute before Hannah spoke.

"You don't look sorry," she teased, lightening the moment considerably.

Camille released Hannah's hand, and picked up her wine. "Well, I'm sorry your trip was," she gave Hannah a small smile, "lacking something. But I'm not sorry that something was me." Her eyes softened over the rim of her glass. "I was thinking about you too." She took a sip of rosé and set the glass on the table.

Hannah's eyes crinkled. "That's good news. It really is. The best news I've heard in a long time."

"I'm glad it makes you happy."

For several minutes they enjoyed their meal without speaking, though Hannah continued to communicate nonverbally beneath the table by stroking Camille's calf with the side of her foot. The song changed to "Under the Bridge" by the Red Hot Chili Peppers.

"Do you know when you're going back to San Francisco?"

The question took Camille by surprise. Hannah confessing an infatuation was one thing, looking ahead to future dates was another gear entirely. "Well, my dad is a lot better now. He only needs me to scoop the litter boxes, and I could hire someone to do that. Also, the Gowear case has been resolved, so there's no concern there."

"It has?" Hannah sounded genuinely relieved. "That's great. I mean, no more conflict of interest, right? Your partnership is safe?"

"It is. I mean, it should be. I haven't gotten the official word yet."

"I'm so relieved." Hannah's eyes softened. "I didn't want to get you in trouble. Bree had me worried about it."

"You talked to Bree about us?"

"Is that okay? I thought because you told Jenna..."

"No, it's fine. What did you tell her?"

"I told her lots of things."

"Like what?"

Hannah's lips curved into the familiar flirty grin, but her cheeks turned an abnormal pink that Camille found intriguing.

"Tell me," she insisted.

Hannah shook her head from side to side until her hair curtained her face. Comically, she blew a few strands out of the way, and peered at Camille through the opening. "I told her that I really like you."

"You did? You do?"

"Yeah."

Camille tried to process the information. Hannah liked her? Not just liked, but *really liked* her, Camille Robbins? How was that even possible? Every lesbian in the Washington metropolitan area was clamoring for a ride on the back of that purple Harley Davidson. Why would Hannah choose Camille? Her mind started to spin. Of course Camille had thought about a relationship with Hannah beyond sex. But she'd sequestered that dream away in her fantasy mind, a place where she'd also won the lottery and lived on the beach with a pack of rescue dogs. Hannah's worried look told Camille she'd let the silence linger too long. She squeezed her fingers.

"I really like you too." Whatever was happening between them wasn't happening to Hannah alone. Camille felt it too.

Hannah tucked her hair behind her ears. The gesture was so endearing Camille longed to kiss her again. "I don't want to weird you out, but ever since I first saw you on the escalator, I haven't been able to stop thinking about you. I usually don't get like this. It's new territory for me."

Camille was confused. "New territory how?"

"Wanting to be with someone more than once."

"You've never slept with a woman more than once?"

"*Of course* I have. I've just never properly dated anyone."

"You want to properly date me?"

"Well, not *too* properly." Hannah slid her foot dangerously into Camille's lap.

"But I live in California."

Hannah shrugged her shoulders as if this were not an issue. "So we'll visit each other a lot."

"That could get expensive."

"Gowear has three corporate jets."

"You said it was your dad's business."

Hannah flashed her flirty smile, the smile that made Camille want to say yes, to whatever she was proposing. "Well, he did give me half the company. Might as well enjoy the perks."

Camille took another sip of wine. "What does Bree think?"

"Bree thinks the music stopped playing when I saw you."

"Please explain."

"According to Bree, we all dance to our own internal music."

"Okay."

"She says I've always been comfortable alone because I never liked anyone else's song more than I liked my own. Also, my music is a bit loud."

Camille laughed. "Is that true?"

"Is my music loud? I'm afraid so. People have been telling me to turn it down my whole life."

"No, the other part. Where you liked my song."

Hannah locked eyes with Camille over the table her expression completely earnest. "Before yesterday I was willing to believe it was all in my head. But then yesterday happened, and it was…"

"Miraculous, stupendous, insane?"

"Right?"

Camille stroked her foot under the table. "Bree sounds really smart. Tell me what else she said."

"She said this was all happening really fast, that I needed to be chill and watch for cues before making any proclamations."

Camille gave her a small smile. "You kind of blew that part."

Hannah shrugged. "Restraint has never been my thing."

"Restraint is way overrated." Camille dropped a hand into her lap and loosened the belt of the bathrobe. Shimmying her shoulders back, she let the garment slip down her back and fall across her lap. Hannah's eyes took in her breasts before drifting happily back up to her face. A low throaty giggle escaped her mouth. "Is this a cue?"

Camille nodded. "What do you think?"

Hannah rose from her chair and offered a hand to Camille. "I think I'm ready for dessert."

Later, after Camille had more than evened the orgasm score and was lying with her back against Hannah's chest in the freestanding, cast-iron, claw-foot tub, she raised the issue of logistics.

"You really think we can make this work?"

"I think we can try." Long arms wrapped loosely around Camille's waist, resting just beneath her breasts. Hannah kissed the back of her neck. "I know it's soon. But your breasts already like me, so there's one hurdle cleared." She rolled Camille's nipples expertly between her thumbs and forefingers.

Camille sucked in a breath and arched her back. "Technically two."

Hannah laughed her throaty giggle. "That's right, two! And this gal…" She slid a hand down to the slickness between Camille's legs. "Well, she's my new best friend."

Camille whimpered as Hannah began to softly stroke her.

"She really does like you." Camille lifted a leg over the side of the tub to allow Hannah better access. "But she…I mean we…I mean I…I, live in California. I know you have planes, and that your fingers are really, really long but…"

Hannah pushed two of the aforementioned fingers deep inside Camille, filling her with delicious pressure. With her other hand she spanned Camille's chest, managing to tease both breasts at once.

"Tell me about my fingers, Camille."

"They're fantastic," was all she could manage as Hannah had begun to lick hot, wet stripes up her neck.

"I think you're fantastic." Hannah bit down on her earlobe. Slowly, she extracted her fingers from Camille's heat, and then plunged them back inside her again.

"Oh, God," Camille groaned and spread her legs wider.

"You make me feel fantastic," Hannah whispered and continued to pump her fingers inside Camille.

Camille trembled as she felt another orgasm begin to build. Hannah seemed to know just how to touch her. Her words were an added aphrodisiac.

"I love fucking you." With each thrust of her hand, Hannah tapped her palm firmly against Camille's clit, causing her to moan. "You're so wet. Even in the water, I can feel how wet you are."

Water splashed around them in the bathtub and onto the floor. Looking down, Camille watched Hannah's fingers thrusting in and out of her. It was like she was the star of her own adult film and the hottest thing she'd ever seen.

"Come for me," Hannah breathed into her ear. "I want to feel it, please? Come for me?"

Camille was not one to make a woman beg. One more thrust of Hannah's hand, and she shattered into a thousand tiny pieces.

"God, Hannah!" She cried out so loudly it echoed off the bathroom walls. Playfully, Hannah moved the hand that had been tending Camille's breasts up to cover her mouth. Camille sucked a finger inside. Holding it gently between her teeth, she rode out the orgasm. As the last spasms rolled through her, she bucked her hips against Hannah's hand, greedy to experience every diminishing pulse.

"I've got you," Hannah dropped her hand from Camille's lips, to hold her securely around the waist.

As the orgasm subsided, Camille covered Hannah's hand with her own, and gently pulled it from her core. Lacing their fingers together, she rested their hands on her stomach, and closed her eyes.

"That was incredible," she said and turned to meet Hannah's lips with her own. Tangling their tongues together she let her know they were not yet done for the evening.

Their earlier activity had displaced much of the water so the bath was no longer full. Hannah was now only half-submerged. Her breasts cresting the surface of the water like a nineteenth-century painting of a mermaid. Camille leaned down and kissed them gently, before pulling away, and leaning against the far end of the tub.

"Where are you going?" Hannah pouted.

"Come and see?" Camille gripped Hannah beneath the knees and pulled her center toward her smiling mouth. The golden eyes darkened with desire.

"Oh, okay," she said shyly. Leaning back on her elbows, Hannah allowed Camille to tug her closer.

Camille studied her prize. "You're so beautiful." She tested Hannah's clit with the tip of her tongue and was rewarded with a low growl.

"You like that?" She swiped her tongue upward through her slit and this time was met with a whimper. Using her fingers, she spread Hannah open and pushed her tongue inside as far as she could.

"Fuck!" Hannah gasped and gripped the side of the tub.

Camille slid her tongue out just a fraction and, using her nose to tease Hannah's clit, began a steady rhythm that soon had them both moaning. Hannah was gushing heat. The juices ran down Camille's chin. She wanted to lap up every drop but dared not pull away lest she miss the main event. When Hannah's legs began to shake, Camille knew she only had moments. Replacing her tongue with two fingers, she sucked Hannah's clit into her mouth and fucked her harder.

Hannah crested her release with a scream. Riding out the orgasm, she reached out a shaky hand and placed it on Camille's head. "Be my girlfriend, please?"

Camille laughed. "You're high on sex." She dragged her tongue once more through Hannah's wet folds drawing a shudder of pleasure.

"I'm high on you."

CHAPTER SEVENTEEN

Leaning In

Hannah drove Camille home on the back of the Harley Davidson. At five thirty a.m., the urban neighborhood was just waking up. Rich smells of breakfast escaped the century-old townhouses, reinforcing the abiding perception of prosperity. Though the sun had begun to rise, headlights were still necessary, and the motorcycle's single bulb flashed ahead of them on the dark street. Watching her cotton dress whip around her legs like a sashaying petticoat, Camille closed her eyes. The tenderness she felt was overwhelming, and yet she wanted more, would take as much as she could get. Miraculously, Hannah seemed to feel the same way.

For the first time, Hannah wasn't wearing black. Dressed in a pair of low-slung, faded blue jeans and a thin white T-shirt that felt impossibly soft against Camille's cheek, she seemed completely at ease. When Camille had offered to Uber home as she'd done the day before, Hannah had declared the idea preposterous. Camille hadn't argued, because she'd understood.

Today wasn't like the day before. Declarations had been made, plans set in motion. They were going to date. It was all terribly grown-up and sophisticated and Camille wanted to twirl in circles like a little girl.

Hannah stopped the bike in front of the Woodley Park house but left the engine running. Camille took off her helmet, but then wrapped her arms more tightly around Hannah and leaned into her back. She needed to go inside and get her day started but couldn't make herself let go.

Hannah took off her helmet, then swiveled her body around to smile at Camille over her shoulder. The scar that ran through her eyebrow was especially noticeable from this angle. Camille reached up to stroke it.

"How did you get this?"

Hannah's eyes closed under the caress. "You mean Simba?"

"Your scar has a name?"

Hannah opened her eyes, and Camille was surprised to see a hint of sadness. "My mom called it that."

"Oh, I'm sorry. We don't have to talk about it."

"That's okay. I want to tell you." Hannah gave Camille a peck on the lips. "I want to tell you all my stories."

"*All* of your stories? Really?"

Hannah laughed. "Okay, maybe not all of them. But I can tell you about Simba." She kissed her again, this time allowing her lips to linger a bit longer before pulling back, kissing her nose and eyelids.

Camille's heart clutched at the gesture. Having a girlfriend was really nice.

"When I was six years old, I fell out of our neighbor's apple tree. I must have snagged a limb on the way down. Because when I hit the ground, my forehead was gushing blood. It took fifteen stitches to sew it up."

"Oh, baby." The endearment slipped out so easily, it was as if Camille had said it a thousand times. Hannah's mouth twitched, but she didn't comment, just continued with the story.

"Apparently, I was very chill throughout the whole thing. I didn't cry in the ambulance or even when the doctor was patching me up. It wasn't until he mentioned a scar that I completely freaked out."

"Why then?"

"I'd just seen the *Lion King*. Scar was the asshole uncle who tricks the cub, Simba, into leaving the pride."

"I remember that."

"Yeah, well I heard the word and lost my mind. I hated that cartoon lion so much for breaking up the family. Mom was all I had and the thought of losing her really scared me. She figured it out right away and told the doctor he was wrong. There would be no scar, but a Simba."

Camille's heart ached for the six-year-old Hannah. "Your mom sounds wonderful."

"She really was."

Camille cupped Hannah's face. Gently, she rubbed her thumb over her eyebrow. "Thanks for telling me about Simba."

"You're welcome." She brushed Camille's lips with her own and Camille melted against her. She knew she should pull away. Their night had been perfect, miraculous but she needed to start her day.

"Can I make you a smoothie?" she heard herself say instead. "I make really great smoothies."

Smoothie? Where was this coming from? Was there even fruit in the house?

In answer, Hannah switched off the engine. Dismounting, she offered a hand to Camille and together they walked to the house. Strong fingers encased her own, calming her, claiming her. Camille waited to feel weird. She hadn't held hands publicly with a lover since law school. Granted it was only six o'clock in the morning, and her father's driveway was a far cry from public, but it felt significant.

Camille was so distracted by Hannah that she forgot about the Kardashians, who rushed the door like Walmart shoppers on Black Friday. Fortunately, Hannah was more than a match for them. When Kim and Kourtney made a break for it, her natural goalie instincts kicked in. She blocked them with her leg, knocking them back into the foyer where they hit the ground like Skittles and scattered behind the partially closed doors of Joe's office. Hannah moved with such quick confidence and athletic grace that Camille couldn't help but be impressed. She was certain her father was still sleeping, so she kept her voice low.

"That was super hot." Camille squeezed her hand.

Hannah shrugged. "It was just instinct."

"Pussy deflecting?" Camille replied, and Hannah laughed out loud. The sound echoed loudly in the entrance hall and Hannah clamped a hand over her own mouth. Her eyes danced in the dim light making Camille want to kiss her again. She wanted to reach out and pull the beautiful body against her own, then strip her down, and stroke her until she melted into a puddle of goo. Something must have shown in her eyes because Hannah's expression changed. Leaning in, she whispered in Camille's ear, "I don't always play defense."

Her sudden nearness caused Camille's knees to go weak. She placed a hand on Hannah's shoulder to steady herself.

"I really want to kiss you right now."

Hannah laughed. "We *are* in the foyer."

Camille thought of Hannah's face when she'd come undone in the entrance hall of the townhouse. She huffed out a breath. "I like that we have a thing."

"Me too."

They locked eyes and, for several seconds, remained motionless, each waiting for the other to give in. Because it was inevitable. Energy crashed around them like a lightning field. Finally, Camille couldn't resist any longer. Looping her hand around Hannah's neck, she pulled her into a heated kiss. Hannah responded by swirling her tongue into Camille's mouth and pressing the hard muscle of her thigh between her legs. A shock of arousal shot straight to Camille's core and her brain fogged with desire. She was close to the point of no return, but it couldn't happen in her father's entrance hall. She wrenched her lips away.

"We can't do this. Not here."

"Upstairs?" Hannah's body radiated heat. Camille swallowed hard, wishing her answer could be different.

"Is it okay if we wait?" She nodded toward the doors leading to her father's office. "My dad's in there, he's probably still sleeping, but I don't want to freak him out."

Hannah's playful expression softened to one of understanding. She loosened her grip on Camille's body, and removed her thigh from between her legs. "Of course it's okay. We have all the time in the world, baby." She took a deliberate step back.

The loving words softened the loss of contact, but just. Camille willed herself to stay strong. "Thank you."

Hannah combed a hand through her beautiful red hair. "I'm actually thinking more about myself." She grinned adorably. "I don't want to have my tongue jammed down your throat the first time I properly meet your dad."

"So it's self-serving?"

"Basically."

"I can respect that." Camille took Hannah's hand, and led her toward the kitchen.

"Smoothie."

"Are you calling me a smoothie?"

"If the shake fits." With her free hand, Hannah reached out and cupped Camille's ass with her strong fingers.

The door swung open to reveal Martina and Joe sitting at the table drinking coffee. Hannah was quick to remove her hand from Camille's backside, but did not drop the hand she was holding. Her father lifted an eyebrow but otherwise did not react. Martina was not so restrained.

"Aha! Good morning Camille." She rose from the table and kissed her on both cheeks. She then addressed Hannah. "And you are Hannah. The one who saved us from drugged cats and then brought flowers. So beautiful! Sit down. I'll make coffee." She gestured to the empty chairs.

"That's okay, Martina. I was just going to fix a smoothie." Camille gestured to Hannah. "Dad, this is my friend, Hannah Richards. Hannah, this is my father, Joe Robbins."

"The girl with the whistle on her phone. I remember you." Joe offered his hand.

Hannah stepped forward to shake it. "It's very nice to meet you. I'm sorry to impose at such an early hour."

"Don't be ridiculous," Joe dismissed the concern with a wave of his hand. "I'm always delighted to meet any friend of Camille's. It happens so rarely, you see. I don't dare complain about the circumstances."

"Dad!" Camille protested, but her father was just warming up. He gestured impatiently for them to sit down, and then turned pointedly to Hannah.

"You, my dear, are a bit of a unicorn. The last time I met a friend of Camille's, who wasn't a work colleague," he paused to wink at Camille, "Clinton was in office."

Camille laughed nervously. Her father was a natural raconteur who liked nothing better than to spin a good yarn. His classes were popular because he both charmed and edified students with witty anecdote-filled lectures. The British accent didn't hurt. Unfortunately, they were not in a media studies class today and the subject at hand was Camille. There was no guessing what he might say. "Stop it, Dad!"

But Hannah was listening intently, which only encouraged him.

"I remember her precisely. The girl was a big fan of the Clinton's cat, Socks."

"That's not true! You were the one who liked that cat." Camille slapped the table. "And that wasn't a friend. She was my piano instructor."

Joe looked genuinely surprised. "Are you sure? You two got on so well together."

"She was in her sixties."

"Ah, you see?" He raised his cup to Hannah. "You are rarer than a unicorn, my dear. Well done."

"Thank you, Mr. Robbins. I take that as a huge compliment." Hannah squeezed Camille's hand under the table. "I'm very happy to have met your daughter."

"You two looked very happy on that motorcycle," Martina said, and calmly set two mugs down on the table. "You want coffee?"

Camille's eyes shot over to the kitchen window where Hannah's Harley sat in full view. A blush crept up her neck. What had her father seen?

"Don't worry, your father didn't see anything," Martina said, following her glance. "His glasses are in the other room." She held a carafe over Hannah's mug waiting for a signal to pour. Hannah smiled pleasantly, her body language betraying nothing beyond the desire for her morning beverage. Martina filled her mug.

"But I tell him everything." She put a hand on her hip and looked down at Camille apologetically. "I'm sorry, but I was so surprised. I just say everything I see."

Camille chanced a look at Hannah whose mouth was twitching with mirth.

"Martina is quite the commentator." Joe Robbins put down his newspaper and studied Hannah intently. "It sounds as if you were kissing the stuffing out of my daughter."

Hannah smiled her sweetest smile, her eyes dancing with merriment. She wasn't the least bit embarrassed to be called out on their public display of affection. "Well, your daughter happens to be very kissable, Mr. Robbins."

"Call me Joe, please." He picked up his coffee cup and took a sip. "Ingrid Bergman once said that kissing is a lovely trick designed by nature to stop speech, when words become superfluous."

"I like that," Hannah replied. She squeezed Camille's hand again. "And it's certainly true. Not that I've run out of things to say to your daughter," she quickly clarified and her eyes slid shyly to Camille's. "But kissing her is a very nice way to communicate too."

"Indeed," Joe agreed, now looking past Hannah to Martina who was boiling eggs on the range. She turned and caught his eye, and it occurred to Camille that Joe's PT wasn't scheduled for another two hours. Martina often stayed after a session but this was the first time she'd come early. Was it possible she stayed the night? Hannah had mistaken the regal Italian woman for Joe's girlfriend when she'd brought the flowers. Could it be true? Camille bit back the question. She'd give Joe Robbins the same courtesy he'd given her. When he was ready to confide in her, she'd be ready to listen.

"I promised you a smoothie," she said instead to Hannah, and rose from the table.

"That's okay." Hannah stood beside her. "I need to get going. Early class today."

"Are you sure?"

"Yeah." Hannah gave her an apologetic look, and took her hand. "But I'd like to spend time with you later, if you're free." Her eyes darkened, letting Camille know exactly how that time might be occupied.

"Okay, text me."

"I will."

"Are you a teacher, Hannah?" Joe asked, his interest piqued. "A student?"

"Teacher. I co-own a climbing gym in Virginia." Camille noticed she didn't mention co-owning Gowear, although it would have undoubtedly impressed both Martina and Joe. "Today I have a class of beginners. They're my favorite," she said, and then smiled. "I love watching their confidence grow as they learn."

She rubbed her thumb over the back of Camille's hand casually. Camille thrilled at the contact. Though she'd had her fair share of sexual partners, being claimed in front of her father, was a completely new experience.

But Joe wasn't interested in their hands. Focused on the conversation, his eyes were alight with understanding.

"Yes!" he agreed. "You've gone straight to the heart of the calling. Watching students learn, coming alive with new information, that's the true reward of teaching."

"Dad's a professor at American University," Camille explained to Hannah.

"I'm taking the semester off," he gestured to his leg, and Hannah gave him a sympathetic smile.

"I heard about the accident. It sounded really bad."

"It was falafel," Joe repeated the tired joke.

Hannah looked confused and Camille patted her arm. "I'll explain later."

"I was a mountain climber in my youth," Martina said, surprising Camille. She had a hard time visualizing the buxom therapist crawling up mountains, but Hannah responded enthusiastically. "That's so cool. There are lots of awesome peaks in Italy."

"Have you been?" Martina wanted to know.

"Oh yes, many times." Hannah smiled at the older woman. "My business partner and I led a climb in the Dolomites last year. It was breathtaking." She turned to Camille. "The catalog cover, remember? We should go sometime."

"Okay."

Martina's intelligent face lit up with recognition. "You are the woman on Camille's computer!"

"I am?" Hannah looked confused, but Camille blushed. She'd been completely busted. Martina was referencing her screen saver. There was no choice but to own it.

"I may use that picture as my screen saver," she confessed.

"Really?" Hannah looked delighted.

"Oh, yes," Martina answered, seemingly unaware of the embarrassment she was causing Camille. "I've seen it many times. The picture is beautiful, but you are so high up, it makes me nervous for your safety. And I used to climb in the Alps."

Hannah was suddenly serious. "We take every precaution to ensure our safety and that of the people climbing with us. I've been a guide for more than ten years and we've never had a serious accident." She turned back to Camille, and her tone softened. "Did you really make it your screen saver?"

"Yes, but I'm sure I'm not the only one," Camille demurred. She looked up shyly to meet Hannah's eye.

"But you're the only one that matters," Hannah replied. Her voice was achingly sweet. Camille desperately wanted to kiss her but managed to restrain herself.

Joe Robbins cleared his throat. "You seem to rock my daughter's world in more ways than one, Hannah."

"Dad!" Camille protested but the spell was broken.

"The feeling is mutual, Joe," Hannah said. "One hundred percent."

CHAPTER EIGHTEEN

Dress Down

Camille willed the Uber driver to be more aggressive. It was nearly eleven o'clock and she needed to get to the office. An ominous email had arrived from Steve Benson. He wanted to see Camille at her earliest convenience but didn't offer a reason. The heading of the email simply read: *Meeting requested.* It was the equivalent of a "See me after class" note. But Camille was not in school and until she was formally named partner, Steve Benson was her boss. Anything routine he would have communicated via email. Her mind searched for reasons why he would need to see her in person.

The delayed morning had her day feeling off-kilter, which was a shame, as it had begun so beautifully. Camille hadn't meant to fall asleep after Hannah left. She was only going to rest her eyes for a bit but had completely passed out. What did she expect? In the past forty-eight hours, she'd taken a new girlfriend, confronted an old lover, and had a scotch-fueled heart-to-heart with a near clone of her younger self. It was all too much. If Khloe and Kim hadn't chased Rob into her bedroom and cornered him inside the armoire, she might have slept all day.

Maybe Benson's unexpected email had to do with the Fabray settlement. Perhaps he'd learned of the settlement and wanted to offer Camille his congratulations. She also couldn't count out the possibility of the partnership announcement. News was expected any day. Perhaps Steve would crack open a bottle of champagne, and tell Camille welcome aboard. But then, why the cryptic email?

She'd texted Jenna, who hadn't a clue. They'd made a plan to meet after work for another debriefing session. Camille couldn't wait to see how big Jenna's eyes got when she told her about Hannah's proclamation. Thinking of her lover, she smiled to herself. No matter what Steve Benson said, it couldn't detract from the fact that Hannah Richards wanted to be her girlfriend.

The Uber driver pulled to a stop in the curved driveway in front of Walker and Jenkins. Camille gathered up her tote and quickly exited the car. She'd emailed Benson's secretary from the Uber and set the appointment for noon. She wanted to get it over as soon as possible, so she could get on with the true agenda of her day—mooning over a beautiful redhead.

She paused to hold the door open for a familiar-looking woman struggling with an infant carrier. Red, white and blue with a curly W on the sunshade, the apparatus resembled something one might bring to a July Fourth parade. Or a Washington Nationals game. Camille looked at the woman again and suddenly knew who she was. It was Beverly Stanley, Nationals fanatic, coming by Walker and Jenkins for a show-and-tell. After nine months with a bun in the oven, she'd brought in the freshly baked goods. Camille had seen this compulsion before. She didn't begrudge new mothers their victory lap but knew if she was ever lucky enough to have a child of her own, the last place she'd want to bring them was a law firm.

She exhaled a sigh of relief. This had to be the reason for the meeting, of course. If Beverly Stanley was dragging her newborn baby around Walker and Jenkins, she was probably getting nostalgic for her old life and wanted her office back. Steve Benson was in charge of assigning offices. He'd want to make sure Camille was okay being downgraded from a partner suite to something more modest. Partners were notoriously touchy about their office status. Benson would only assume Camille would be too. She pushed the issue from her mind.

She opened her office door to find Lillian waiting for her amidst the bobbleheads. Camille hadn't seen her since she'd departed the Woodley Park house two nights ago half-drunk. She'd emailed the young associate Cory's good news but had heard nothing back. Yesterday Lillian had taken a well-advised personal day. Camille had wondered if she might not come back at all. But now she was here, acting as if nothing had happened. Dressed as usual in a beautifully tailored suit, the only difference was that she'd swapped her three-inch heels for a modest flat.

Despite her confusion, Camille smiled. "Nice shoes."

Lillian rotated her foot in a circle. "And I can actually walk in them."

"Good for you." Camille sat down behind the desk and began stacking files. If she was leaving Nats' Park, she might as well begin packing up. She searched for something to say. "Did you see my email? We should have the papers today." She looked at Lillian, but the young woman was studying her own fingernails as if checking for a flaw in the manicure.

"Lillian?"

"I did see the email. That's great news."

"Uh, yeah."

Camille narrowed her eyes. If she wasn't there to discuss Gowear, then why was Lillian in her office? After their frank discussion at the kitchen table, maybe it was best to go straight to the point. "Did you talk things out with Mia? I spoke with her yesterday, and she made it clear that reconciliation is what she wants. I think she truly loves you."

Lillian's face split into a huge grin, making her look about sixteen. "I know. She told me last night." She flexed her left hand in Camille's direction.

Camille gaped at the rose-cut diamond on Lillian's ring finger. Flanked by slightly smaller emeralds, it was an exquisite piece of jewelry.

"Is that what I think it is?"

Lillian nodded solemnly but her eyes shone with happiness.

"Mia asked me to marry her." She paused to gauge the effect the news had on Camille, before continuing. "We have to keep it a secret until she leaves the firm, but after that, she's promised to tell everyone."

The sight of the engagement ring rendered Camille temporarily speechless. When she and Mia were together, marriage had never crossed her mind. Though Camille had been in love with Mia and craved the legitimacy of a public relationship, she'd never once considered becoming her wife. She searched her mind for residual hurt and found nothing. She was over Mia and had been for a long time.

Lillian was watching her closely, waiting for a reaction. Camille reached over to pat her arm. "Congratulations, I mean it."

The younger woman gave her a relieved smile. "Thank you. That means a lot to me. To us," she corrected herself. "And I know you had something to do with it. Mia told me about your talk…"

"So, Mia's really leaving the firm?" Camille moved on to the next salient point.

Lillian nodded. "Yes. She talked to Jason Tabor about going in-house at Gowear. He loves the idea. She's negotiating with them right now. But it's just a formality. Mia says it's a done deal."

"Wow, I don't know what to say." Camille tried to process the news. "I can't believe Mia is leaving the firm. It's been her entire career."

"I know. She told me she's taking the job so we can be together." A dreamy look came over Lillian's face. "She doesn't want to stand in the way of my chance of making partner one day. Can you believe it?"

Camille thought of Mia huddled beneath her desk, blubbering like a three-year-old child lost in a shopping mall. "Yes, I can actually." She smiled in spite of herself. "I'm glad it all worked out for you. I really am."

"I was nervous about telling you."

Camille held up a hand. "Trust me, I'm fine. My issue right now is packing up this office."

Lillian was surprised. "Are you going back to California? Is your dad well enough? I thought you needed to stay longer?"

Camille was touched by the note of concern in her voice. Lillian seemed like a truly nice person. Under different circumstances, they might have been friends.

"Not California, just yet," Camille said, continuing to stack the files, "But I may be moving to another office in the building. I ran into Beverly Stanley in the lobby. I think she's coming back early from maternity leave."

Lillian looked confused. "Did she tell you that?"

"No, but Steve Benson wants to see me. I just put two and two together."

"I don't think that's it."

"Why not?"

"I just saw Beverly. She's in love with that baby. All she talked about was Nathaniel's bowel movements and feeding schedule. She didn't say anything about coming back."

"Please tell me she didn't name that child Nathaniel."

Lillian barked a laugh. "They're calling him Natty."

Camille shook her head. If Beverly Stanley wasn't coming back early, then why did Benson want to see her? A new bloom of worry began to grow. Could word have gotten back to someone at the firm that Camille was involved with a client? It certainly wasn't out of the question. DC was a small town. How many people had seen Hannah declare herself at Molly's Diner?

"What's wrong?" Lillian asked.

"Nothing." Camille waved her hand. Just because she was warming to Lillian didn't mean she would confide her feelings about Hannah. Lillian was Mia's fiancé after all and might go telling tales. Things had a way of leaking out in bed.

"Can you do me a favor and see if the FedEx has come in yet?"

Lillian took the bait. "Sure."

"That would be great. Tabor seemed pretty anxious to have it behind him."

"I'll go check right now."

"Thanks, and really, congratulations again on your engagement."

"Thank you." Lillian smiled at her. "I'll make sure to tell Mia."

"You do that." Camille tried her best to sound sincere, but knew she'd failed miserably. Being over Mia and wishing her eternal happiness were two completely separate things. Fortunately, Lillian was too blissed out to notice. She left the office humming Mendelssohn's "Wedding March."

Camille watched the door close, then glanced at her phone to check the time. The meeting was scheduled in five minutes. She slid the HR letter detailing Mia's transgressions out of her briefcase and into a file folder. Now that Mia was jumping ship to Gowear corporate, Camille was almost certain she wouldn't need to use it. But you never knew. Mia had thrown her curve balls before, and Camille needed to be prepared for anything. If the Washington Nationals catcher's mask wasn't mounted to the wall, she might be tempted to take that too.

A few minutes later she was outside Benson's door, poised to knock.

"He's waiting for you, Ms. Robbins," a voice behind her said. "Ms. Shannon is already inside. Can I get you a cup of coffee? A glass of water?"

Camille stopped short. What was Mia doing in Benson's office? Hadn't Lillian just said she was at Gowear corporate negotiating her employment contract? Camille smiled pleasantly at the managing partner's secretary. She was tempted to ask for a shot of scotch.

"I'm fine, thank you," she lied and tried to steady her nerves. There was no way this was good news. Taking a deep breath, she rapped lightly on the door, and then pushed it open.

"Camille, hello."

Steve Benson was seated behind a massive walnut desk that looked as if it might have come with the building. His office was enormous, even bigger than Beverly Stanley's, though case files stacked on every available surface made it feel crowded. Mia sat in a chair facing Benson's desk. She did not turn to greet Camille and seemed wholly absorbed with something in her lap. It was not a good sign.

"Hi, Steve. Hello, Mia." Camille decided to take the high road. Until she knew what the meeting was about, she wouldn't jump to conclusions. Mia didn't respond to her greeting but continued looking at the thing she was holding. *What was going on?*

"Have a seat, please Camille. Just slide those files on the floor." Benson gestured to a chair opposite Mia, stacked high with manila folders. Awkwardly Camille sloughed the files off the chair and into an unbalanced pile next to the desk.

"Is this okay?"

"Sure, anywhere. That's fine." Benson waved his hand dismissively and Camille swallowed hard. The last time she'd been in his office he'd plied her with magic coffee beans. Now he didn't even have a chair for her to sit in? Her blood ran cold when she saw what Mia was looking at.

"Something's come to our attention, Camille. Something I'd like to clear up."

"Okay." Camille took a deep breath. She dared not look at Mia's lap again.

"Beverly Stanley was here this morning. She found an odd file in her office that has us all confused."

"That's a nice word for it, Steve," Mia cut in, venom dripping from every syllable. She held up the black folder Jenna had prepared on Hannah as if it was the smoking gun in the Kennedy assassination.

Shit. Shit. Shit.

"What word would you use, Mia?" the managing partner asked, stoking the fire. Camille got the impression he was enjoying himself.

"Incriminating?" Mia's eyes sparked dark with hellfire. Camille had never seen her so angry. She looked at the folder and shook her head.

"This is not what it looks like," she said lamely.

"What does it look like?" Benson was calm and Camille knew to tread lightly. He and Mia were both excellent attorneys. Any misstep could be twisted into a weapon and used against her. The truth was the only way to go.

"That I've assembled a fact-finding file on Mia's client."

"Fact-finding including all their financials?" Mia hissed. "You are trying to poach the account."

"I most certainly have no intention of doing that," countered Camille.

Mia slammed her hand down on the folder. "Then what the hell is this?"

"Hannah Richards and I are dating," Camille replied and watched Mia's mouth flatten into thin line. "A friend of mine put that together as a joke. If you look through it, you can see for yourself. There's lots of fangirl stuff in there." Camille's arguments trailed away as Mia opened the section Jenna had compiled on Gowear's financials. She swallowed hard. Page after official-looking page listed all the company's assets and debts, the salaries of the top executives, stock option vesting schedules, everything. Jenna had left no meat on the bone. It was all in the folder.

"Explain this."

"It's just overkill. My friend went too far. Hannah and I are dating. That's it."

"You're delusional," Mia spat. She turned to the managing partner. "Hannah Richards is not exactly known for her exclusivity." When she looked back at Camille, the black eyes were now patronizing. "You've been in DC, what? Three weeks? I'm not doubting that you've slept with her." Slowly, she turned the pages of the folder, showcasing the parade of woman Hannah had squired to private events. "But if you think you're anyone special, Camille, I'm afraid you're sadly mistaken." She handed the file to Benson and sat back in her chair.

"Ultimately, it's your call Steve. But, I think it's pretty clear what's going on. Ms. Robbins made a play for my client, hoping to gain her business. We all know Camille hasn't any clients of her own. Did you think this would secure the partnership?"

"No, because it's not true." Camille kept her voice steady though her gut was churning. "I didn't know Hannah was co-owner of Gowear until after we'd met. I have no interest in their business. I only want the girl." She arched an eyebrow at Mia who glared back at her. "But we can clear this up right now." She took her phone from her briefcase. "Shall I call Hannah?"

"Oh, I'm sure she already knows," Mia countered. "When I met with Jason Tabor earlier this morning, he promised to fill her in on everything. He's a very protective father, you see."

Camille felt the color drain from her face. The thought of Hannah learning about the file before she could fill her in felt like a punch in the stomach. She remembered how touched she'd been that morning to learn that Camille had used her picture as a screen saver. Now she'd think she was a stalker.

There was nothing for Camille to do but fight back. She hadn't worked this hard for her partnership, toiled long hours, sacrificed her social life, to lose everything over a lie. "Then you also know that Lulu Fabray signed the settlement. We expect to get the papers this afternoon."

"Yes, I heard," Mia sneered. "Lillian told me you sent your assistant to harass the plaintiff. It was a complete breach of protocol and might have jeopardized the settlement. Do you expect us to congratulate you?"

"It worked." Camille had no other excuse. She turned imploringly to Benson. "Sometimes you go the extra mile for a client."

"Like when you're trying to poach them?" Mia tapped her finger on the folder.

Camille shook her head. "It's not like that."

"I disagree."

"Ladies." Benson was enjoying the exchange far more than was warranted. Camille wondered if he was aware of her past relationship with Mia, and decided he probably was. It was likely everyone in the law firm had known.

"I'll review this with the other partners, and we'll let you know our decision."

"Decision?"

"Regarding your partnership offer. Poaching a client is a serious allegation. It won't be taken lightly."

"I haven't done anything wrong."

"Then you've got nothing to worry about."

CHAPTER NINETEEN

Truth Be Told

Camille ignored the doorbell. Martina was doing physical therapy with Joe and would answer it. It wasn't part of her job description but Martina was now more like a member of the family. That afternoon she'd even scooped the cat boxes. Camille simply hadn't been up for the task. She'd come home from work, told Martina and Joe the story of the file in Beverly Stanley's office, and then fallen into bed. Now she could barely lift her head from the pillow.

All afternoon she'd tried to contact Hannah. She'd called her cell phone, the gym. She'd texted her repeatedly, but there had been no response. The silence was deafening, so loud Camille could barely hear her own thoughts. She worried Hannah was sending the ultimate message by not communicating—that she believed Mia's interpretation of the black folder, and written Camille off as unscrupulous. It did look bad. At the very best Camille looked like a stalker. She glanced at her phone lying silently next to her on the bed. At least if Hannah called her back she would be able to explain. To be found guilty, without having a chance to present her case, was making Camille physically ill.

The only calls she'd received that day were from Jenna. In fact, she'd been blowing up her phone for the past hour. The texts were coming in every five minutes like planes at National Airport, but Camille hadn't opened any of them. Jenna would feel awful when she learned of the fallout created by her research. She'd go to Steve Benson and confess everything. He might even believe her, but it wouldn't get Hannah back. What they had together was too fragile. It was like a newborn colt, standing for the first time. Given the proper time and nurture, it had the potential to grow into something magnificent. Strike a blow this early, and it would never find its legs at all.

Camille heard voices at the door, followed by light footsteps tapping quickly up the stairs. Instantly, she was on alert. Martina rarely ventured to the second floor and had a much heavier gait. Whoever was on the stairs was taking them two at a time. Seconds later, there was a light rap on her door.

"Camille? Are you in there?" There was a brief pause, followed by more knocking. It was louder this time, more insistent. The handle turned but caught on the lock.

"Open the door Cam-o-flage, I need to talk to you."

"Jenna?"

"Who the fuck else? I've been calling you for hours. Open the door." She jiggled the handle.

Camille sighed as she crossed the room. Jenna must have heard about the ill-fated meeting. What did Camille expect? As a former paralegal, Jenna knew everyone in the office and craved gossip more than baked goods. If Benson's secretary had told anyone about the meeting, Jenna the Antenna would have caught wind of it.

She slid back the bolt and twisted the handle. Pulling open the door, she found a wild-eyed Jenna sporting equally wild hair. The springy curls stood out in all directions.

"Why didn't you answer my texts? What is wrong with you?" Jenna stood in the doorway, wringing her hands.

Camille was confused. "I thought you knew."

"Knew what?"

"They found the file."

"The file, what file?"

"The information you put together on Hannah. Beverly Stanley found it in her office and gave it to Mia."

Jenna blinked hard.

"That's what the Benson meeting was about. Mia formally accused me of trying to steal Gowear as a client from her. My partnership is now under review."

Jenna reacted as if physically struck. The mad energy in her eyes, present only moments before, clouded over like fog on a mirror. Even her hair seemed to deflate.

"You didn't know?" If Jenna wasn't aware of the Gowear drama, then why was she here?

"No, I didn't." She sat down hard on Camille's bed, as if she didn't trust her legs to bear the weight of the information. "I've been out of the office all day at meetings. I had no idea. I'm so sorry, Camille."

Camille was confused. "Then why have you been calling me? Why are you here?"

Jenna laid the back of her hand over her eyes. "Did you read *any* of my texts?"

"No." Camille sat down next to her friend. "I've been trying to get in touch with Hannah all afternoon. Mia told Jason Tabor about the file and I'm pretty sure he told Hannah. They think I was only sleeping with her to get Gowear as my own client." She lay down next to Jenna. "Hannah won't answer the phone or text me back. I don't know what to do."

"That's because she's in the hospital," Jenna said quietly.

"What?" Camille turned her head on the bed. She wasn't sure she'd heard correctly.

"If you'd read my texts you'd know everything." Jenna propped herself on one elbow. Looking down at Camille, she shook her head. "A student made a mistake. He forgot to tie-in his rope or something and fell on Hannah. Knocked her unconscious. An ambulance brought her to the ER at Fairfax Hospital. Melissa called me immediately. I've been trying to reach you ever since."

"What? No!" Camille leapt from the bed. All concerns about the partnership flew from her head at the thought of Hannah in distress. She fired off questions as they came to mind. "How is she now? Did she wake up? Please tell me she's okay."

"I wish I could." Jenna rubbed at her forehead. "The last time I spoke with Melissa, Hannah was still out cold."

"We have to go there." Camille was on autopilot. She pushed her feet into already-laced Converse and grabbed Jenna's hand. "Can you drive me? Do you have your car?"

"It's outside." Jenna stood up too slowly for the pace of Camille's racing heart.

"What's the matter with you? Why are you being so slow? Do I need to call a cab?"

Jenna hung her head. "I can't believe I fucked up your partnership."

"It's not important." Camille tried to drag Jenna toward the door but she stopped short on the threshold, refusing to budge.

Her eyes shone with remorse. "How can you say that? You've worked so hard for this."

Camille squeezed her hand. Everything had suddenly become very clear. The file drama definitely sucked, but it would almost certainly unravel to nothing. Camille hadn't done anything wrong. Hannah could attest to that when she woke up. It was just as she'd told Benson in the meeting, Camille didn't want the business, she wanted the girl. But right now, she wanted a ride to the hospital. Camille took Jenna's hand.

"There's nothing we can do about it right now. I know you're sorry, but if you really want to help me, you'll give me a ride to the hospital. I need to make sure Hannah's okay. Do you think you can drive?"

The pep talk had its desired effect. Jenna bobbed her head and, without further protest, followed Camille out of the bedroom and down the stairs. Martina and Joe were waiting by the front door.

"The cats are locked in my office," Joe offered, waving a crutch. His normally jovial voice was noticeably solemn.

"Thank you, Dad." Camille put her hand on the doorknob.

"Yes, well, Jenna told us about Hannah's accident. The last thing you needed was a game of Kardashian tennis."

"I appreciate it." She touched his arm.

"And here is your dinner."

Martina deposited a large paper bag into Jenna's hands, as if fulfilling a previously placed to-go order. Jenna shot Camille a questioning look, but her arms closed protectively around the bag.

"Thank you." Camille smiled at Martina and then twisted the doorknob. There was no arguing with the therapist about the food, and who knew how long they would be at the hospital?

"Let us know when you know something?"

Camille managed a weak smile. "I will."

Minutes later, they were in the Mini Cooper racing toward Rock Creek Parkway. Jenna steered the low-slung roadster through traffic like a NASCAR driver. If Camille hadn't been preoccupied with Hannah's welfare, she might have been impressed. But her thoughts were only of the woman in the hospital. She desperately wanted to know that she was okay. It was as if Jenna could read her mind.

"We'll be there in twenty-five minutes, thirty at the most." She gunned the vehicle forward, passing a car hugging the left lane. "This is the fastest route. Before we moved out of the city, I sometimes drove Melissa in on late-night calls." Jenna's chatter was a transparent attempt to distract Camille. "You know how she has a hard time waking up."

"I do." Camille felt tears prick the back of her eyes. *What if Hannah didn't wake up?* The thought filled her with unexpected emotion. It was preposterous. She barely knew the woman. Yes, they'd connected. They'd had wonderful conversations and amazing sex, talked of exploring a future together. But it was all still just raw potential. Wasn't it? Why did it feel like so much more? Why did it feel like they couldn't get to the hospital fast enough?

The miles melted away in silence. As they passed into the Northern Virginia suburbs, Camille began to see directional signs for Fairfax Hospital. She tried to steady herself by taking a deep breath, but it didn't work. How would she explain her knowledge of Hannah's accident without getting Melissa into trouble? You didn't have to be an expert in hospital ethics to know giving patient information to non-family members was a violation of privacy. No one from the family had called Camille. After Mia's disclosure that morning, Jason Tabor was likely to have put Camille on the do-not-admit list.

Jenna pulled into the hospital's parking garage and found a miracle spot near the elevators. She turned off the engine and pulled out her phone. Checking the screen, she let out a loud whoop. "Okay! Good news. Melissa says there's not even a concussion. Hannah's expected to wake up any time." She looked up smiling. "Oh, and this was from an hour ago. Melissa's on rounds now. Hannah may already be conscious."

Camille gave her friend a tentative smile. It was hard not to get caught up in her enthusiasm. She wanted so much to believe Hannah was going to be okay. But she didn't want to jinx the recovery by celebrating prematurely. What if something else was going on? Jenna must have sensed her hesitation. Exiting the car, she held the phone so Camille could read the text herself.

"This is good news."

"I know. I just really wish I could see her."

The large brown eyes narrowed to half moons. "Why can't you? When Melissa is done with rounds she can give us Hannah's room number." She glanced back at her phone. "It should be really soon."

Camille shook her head. "Think about it. I'm not a family member. How am I even supposed to know about Hannah's accident much less her room number? I don't want to get Melissa into trouble."

"Oh, shit." Jenna had clearly not considered the breach of protocol.

"Yeah." Camille pressed her palms down on the roof of the car. "I'm not sure what to do here."

"You could say I called you," a voice behind them suggested. Jenna and Camille turned to see Hannah's business partner, Bree, walking toward them from the elevator. "I don't know who Melissa is, but I'd hate for her to get into trouble."

"Melissa is my wife," Jenna said automatically.

"Oh, well then we definitely don't want her in trouble." Bree smiled pleasantly at them both.

Why was she acting so calm? Had Hannah's condition changed?

"No, we don't." Jenna studied her. "Who are you, please?"

Camille remembered her manners. "Jenna, this is Bree. She's Hannah's business partner." To her own ear, Camille's voice sounded steadier than she felt.

Jenna was quick to catch on. "Ah, someone who would know about her accident."

"I also know her room number." Bree smiled again, this time showing a dimple.

Why was Bree so happy?

"If you want to wait a minute, I'll walk you there myself. It'll make you look even more legit." She winked at Camille. "I just need to get Hannah's phone out of my car."

"Hannah's phone?"

"Yeah, she's been asking for it, said she needed to check in with someone." Bree winked at her again.

"Hannah's awake?" Camille heard her own voice crack and placed a hand over her mouth as if she could hold the pieces together.

"I thought you knew." Bree's face clouded with concern. She walked forward and placed a hand on Camille's arm. Camille was surprised at the gesture of familiarity until she felt the tears on her cheeks. Bree gave her arm a light squeeze. "I should have said so immediately. Hannah came to about forty-five minutes ago and hasn't shut up since. She was singing the theme song to the *Fresh Prince of Bel-Air* when I left the room just now. She's going to be fine."

"Really?"

Bree nodded. She squeezed Camille's arm again.

"I'm so glad she's okay," Camille said, blinking back tears.

"It takes more than a flying dentist to take Hannah down."

"She got hit by a dentist?" Jenna asked.

"And lived to tell the tale."

"I'm so glad she's okay," Camille repeated.

She swiped at the tears with the back of her hand, but only managed to smear them across her face. "I'm sorry. I don't know why I'm crying. I'm just so glad she's okay. You probably think I'm ridiculous."

"I think Hannah is lucky to have someone who cares about her so much," Bree said before letting go of her arm as Jenna moved in to gather Camille in a protective hug.

"I've got this."

"Great." Bree gave way without a fight. "I'll grab Hannah's phone, and then we can all go up together."

"I'm just so glad she's okay," Camille said like a broken record. Jenna's head only reached Camille's collarbone and she let her tears fall unchecked into her friend's soft curls. *Hannah was awake. She was going to be okay.*

"You're getting me all wet, and not in a good way," Jenna protested, but made no move to push her away.

Camille hiccup laughed and let her friend go. She needed to compose herself. If she was going to visit Hannah in her hospital room, possibly come face-to-face with Hannah's father, she needed some semblance of control. She searched her bag for a tissue but came up empty.

"Okay, ready." Bree was back from the car. In one hand she held Hannah's phone, the other a package of travel tissues. She handed the tissues to Camille.

As they waited for the elevator, Camille did her best to clean her face. She was stunned by the intensity of emotion she was feeling. She hadn't realized how tightly she'd been holding on to hope, until she'd been allowed to relax her grip. Now her body was reacting in a way that she didn't recognize, a common occurrence when Hannah was involved. The elevator opened in front of them, and the three women entered the car. Bree pushed the button marked four. Jenna pressed two. She looked up at Camille, her large eyes cautious.

"Is it okay if I find Melissa first? I want to update her on Hannah's condition and talk to her about some other stuff." She handed Camille the keys to the Mini Cooper. "If you need to bolt. I can get a ride home."

Camille nodded. "That's fine." She knew by other stuff Jenna meant the file on Hannah. Jenna felt awful about the situation she'd created and craved the comfort of her partner. It was all a big mess, but something they could deal with later. What mattered right now was that Hannah was okay. Camille dropped the car keys in her bag. The elevator stopped on the second floor and she gave Jenna a quick hug.

"I'll text you."

"Okay. Good luck. Goodbye, Bree."

"It was nice meeting you."

The door closed and the elevator continued its ascent. "You came at a good time," Bree informed her. "Jason and Stacey were about to get dinner. You should have Hannah all to yourself for a little while."

"I'm just so glad she's okay," Camille repeated the only thought in her head, and felt a fresh wave of emotion overtake her. She mopped at her face. "What's wrong with me?" She muttered under her breath.

Bree surprised her by laughing out loud. "I'm not sure. But whatever it is, I think it's contagious."

"Why do you say that?"

"Because Hannah has the same damn thing."

CHAPTER TWENTY

The Extra Mile

The door to Hannah's hospital room stood slightly ajar. A light was on inside, but no sounds came from within. Bree knocked once before entering the room. "Hey, Hannah? Up for company?"

Camille braced herself for the bolt of recognition she always got when she saw Hannah. But the bed was empty and Camille felt a keen letdown instead. She looked around for evidence of Hannah but found nothing. If this was her room, she wasn't in it.

"She must be in the bathroom." Bree knocked on the door to the en suite. "Heads-up Hannah, someone's here to see you." She turned and smiled at Camille, then rapped on the door again. "Hannah?" She tried the handle. Finding it unlocked, she pushed it open. The bathroom was also empty.

"I'm not sure what's going on. Hannah was here when I left a few minutes ago." Bree's pixie face knit into an expression of concern.

"Maybe we're in the wrong room," Camille offered hopefully. She didn't want to consider alternative possibilities.

Bree pointed to the dry erase board opposite the bed. Hannah Richards was clearly printed in black ink.

"Let me go find the nurse. Maybe she'll know what's going on."

"Is someone sick?"

At the sound of the familiar voice Camille turned and saw Hannah standing in the doorway. Her red hair was flattened against her head as if she'd just taken off her motorcycle helmet. Otherwise, despite the faded hospital gown and bright green slip-proof socks, she looked completely normal. In each hand she held a small container of single-serving applesauce.

Bree exhaled loudly. "Dude! Where did you go? Why are you out of bed? I told you I was getting your phone." She held up the device. "You had Camille very worried."

Hannah looked genuinely concerned. "I did?"

The warmth of her expression washed over Camille like a tropical wave. If Hannah knew about the black folder, she didn't care.

"I'm sorry, baby. I was just hungry." Hannah held up the applesauce. Her mouth slid into the irresistible flirty smile, drawing Camille's eyes to her lips. *Baby.* She wondered when it would be okay to kiss her. She knew she was staring but didn't care. Hannah was okay. She was standing right in front of Camille holding tiny containers. It was all that mattered.

"I'm just so glad you're okay."

"She keeps saying that." Bree put Hannah's phone on the hospital table, near the bed. She nodded toward the applesauce. "I thought your dad was bringing you food."

"I couldn't wait."

Camille thought of the to-go bag Martina had prepared for them. "There's food in Jenna's car."

"What kind of food? Can you please be more specific?" Hannah's tone was mock serious. God, she was pretty. "I mean, food from Jenna's car doesn't have the most appetizing ring. You could never name a restaurant that."

"No." Camille couldn't help smiling back. "It would be a horrible name for a restaurant. Martina packed us a dinner. I think it's baked ziti." Camille fished Jenna's keys out of her purse. "I'm not sure what else is in the bag, but I'm happy to go get it."

Hannah's head swiveled comically to Bree, who let out a breath.

"I see where this is going." Bree plucked the keys from Camille's hand and then wagged a finger between the two of them, as if she were a teacher leaving a classroom unattended. "I'll be back in ten minutes. Don't get into any trouble."

"Thanks, Breezy. I owe you." Hannah held out a container of applesauce. "Snack for the road?"

"Tempting, but no," Bree said and left the room, thoughtfully closing the door behind her. Hannah dropped the snack containers on the table next to her cell phone and moved purposefully toward Camille. Closing the distance quickly, she pulled Camille into a warm embrace. It was unbelievable. An hour ago, Hannah had been unconscious. Now she was standing here, not only in control of her own mind and body, but of Camille's as well.

"Thank you for coming," she murmured into Camille's ear, stirring her passion. Camille steeled herself to resist. No matter how desperately she wanted to make out with Hannah in this hospital room, it wasn't a good idea. There was probably some kind of rule about it. Camille clasped her hands together behind Hannah's back to keep them from wandering.

"I was really worried about you." She pulled back to look at her properly.

"I got hit by a dentist," Hannah joked. She leaned in to brush her lips sweetly against Camille's.

"I'm sorry. I just really needed to do that."

"Don't apologize." Camille smiled and promptly began to cry again. *What was the matter with her?*

"Hey, it's okay. Oh, baby, come here." Hannah pulled Camille tightly against her body. The feeling of the embrace shifted from sexual to protective. Camille gasped into her hair.

"I was really worried about you," she repeated, but knew it was more than that. It was clear that Hannah had yet to be told about Mia's allegation. The notion that Camille had used Hannah to secure her partnership might be their undoing. The folder, coupled with the screen saver, might create enough smoke to choke their fledgling romance. How could Hannah not be suspicious of Camille's motives?

Camille thought of the frog on the purple motorcycle, and a fresh wave of tears washed over her. *Would that be used against her too?* It had been a lovely coincidence. A sign from her mother. It wasn't fair. She gulped in a breath and felt Hannah's arms tighten around her.

"It was just a dumb accident." Hannah stroked Camille's hair, as if comforting a child. "Gerald's an experienced climber. I trained him myself. He just got sloppy today. Forgot to tie-in. When he started to rappel down the wall, he fell on top of me. Thank God, he's vegan. Only weighs about nine pounds." Camille knew Hannah was making light of the situation, but she didn't know the half of it.

"That's awful." To Camille's horror, the tears did not abate. If anything, the comfort of Hannah's body, the feeling of being held in her strong arms, released a fresh wave of emotion.

"Better me than another client," Hannah joked and Camille hiccupped.

"Hey, it's okay." Gently she rocked Camille from side to side.

They might have stayed that way forever had they not been interrupted by an indignant nurse, who chased Hannah back into bed with threats of calling her ward supervisor. She then took Hannah's vitals and left the room with promises to track down her clothes.

"I don't know why they had to strip me naked for a head injury." Hannah plucked at the soft, cotton fabric of the hospital gown.

"Maybe they couldn't pass up the opportunity. I know I'd have a hard time," Camille quipped and Hannah brightened.

"Hey! You made a joke. A sexy joke about seeing me naked." She beamed her brightest smile, and the golden eyes sparkled, happily. "Does this mean you're feeling better?"

Camille bit her lip. This was the time to tell Hannah about the issue at Walker and Jenkins. It would be better to share the information before Jason Tabor did. He was almost certain to be angry. The idea that someone would toy with the emotions of his only child for professional gain was despicable. Until the first flush of outrage subsided, the fact that it wasn't true, would be beside the point.

Camille wished she could fast-forward to the time when everything had been resolved. She hated the thought of putting any doubt into a heart that at present was open to loving her. What if Hannah didn't understand?

"I'm feeling a bit better, thanks," Camille hedged, and leaned in to press her lips against Hannah's. She needed to convey all she was feeling into this one action. It might be the last time she was allowed access, so she gave it everything she had.

Hannah's lips parted in surprise, and Camille felt her smile before she returned the kiss in full. Her hands moved automatically to cradle Camille's head and she held her firmly in place. Their tongues stroked each other gently as, once more, fire threatened to ignite between them. Coming up for air, Camille pressed her forehead into Hannah's and whispered, "I just can't seem to get enough of you." She kissed her again.

Hannah's arms slipped around her waist, and she pulled Camille down so she was almost lying on top of her. "That's not a problem for me."

"Well it's a problem for me."

Camille froze at the sound of the male voice in the room. Hannah stopped kissing her but didn't relax her grip.

"Hi, Dad." She smiled into Camille's eyes, like a naughty teenager caught after curfew. It was clear she thought her father's concern centered solely on her physical well-being. She'd no idea the true nature of his objections.

"I'd like to talk to you."

"Relax, Dad. I'm fine," Hannah protested, still not releasing her hold on Camille. "This is my girlfriend Camille, by the way."

"We've met." The gravity of his tone put his daughter on notice.

With some effort, Camille pushed out of Hannah's embrace, and sat back on the bed. Hannah followed her halfway up, then propped herself on an elbow. "What's going on?"

"Some serious allegations were brought to my attention this morning." Jason Tabor's deep voice resonated with regret. He clearly didn't relish the role of messenger.

"I don't understand. What's going on?" Hannah's mouth tipped up into an uncertain smile. She turned her head toward Camille.

"It's all a misunderstanding." Camille addressed Jason Tabor directly. "I know Mia talked to you this morning, Mr. Tabor. I know the situation looks bad. But it's not what you think it is, I promise." She kept her fingers firmly entwined with Hannah's, squeezing them at intervals for emphasis.

"What do I think it is?" Jason Tabor kept a poker face. He'd not risen to the top of his industry by showing his hand too soon. He approached the bed and held out a bottle of boutique spring water and a banana to Hannah. "Stacey's waiting for our takeout in the lobby. I didn't want to leave you alone too long." He eyed Camille. "Now I'm glad I didn't."

"What's going on?" Hannah asked again and pushed herself up to a fully seated position. "What are you two talking about?"

Jason Tabor shot Camille a challenging look. "Ms. Robbins? My daughter wants to know what's going on. Would you care to explain?"

"Yes." Camille took a deep breath. "I'd care very much to explain." She kept a firm grip on Hannah's hand, thankful she hadn't pulled away. If anything, Hannah had applied firmer pressure against Camille's palm, signaling her solidarity. Camille's heart clutched at the show of trust. She hoped the information revealed in the next few minutes wouldn't cause that trust to disappear.

"Mia gave you the wrong idea," Camille began, and knew it sounded weak.

Hannah gave her an encouraging look and squeezed her hand.

"Just tell us the truth," Hannah's father urged, a firm edge to his voice.

"The truth is I met Hannah on an escalator."

"You were singing," Hannah prompted and Camille smiled.

"I had no idea who she was. I promise. Then I saw her again, the same day, and we started talking."

"I thought Camille was really pretty," Hannah added. She was clearly trying to be helpful. Despite the circumstance, Camille's smile grew wider.

"At first I only saw her on the escalator. But we kept running into each other."

"I may have figured out your schedule," Hannah admitted, and Camille laughed.

"But I changed my schedule, to run into you. I normally go in at six a.m."

"Really?"

"Yes." They smiled sweetly at each other for a moment before Camille picked up the story again.

"Then I saw Hannah at the Gowear party."

"You're the girl she ran off with?" Hannah's father shook his head, processing the aha moment.

"Flew off with," Camille corrected.

"It was awesome," Hannah reminisced.

"When I learned of Hannah's affiliation with Gowear, I immediately informed her there was a conflict of interest."

"And I laughed in her face."

Hannah was defiant. She tossed back her beautiful red hair, daring her father to object. Camille imagined she'd looked like this when facing down a penalty kick.

"But then I kissed her," Hannah continued, before pausing to think. "Or she kissed me. I can't remember." She gazed dreamily at Camille. Hannah was enjoying their walk down memory lane, so Camille stayed in step.

"I kissed you."

"Really?"

"I'm pretty sure."

Camille turned to Hannah's father. "There was less than a twenty-hour overlap of my knowing about the conflict of interest and the case being resolved. Lulu has signed the papers, by the way."

Jason Tabor looked away but Hannah cocked her head to the side, again calling to mind a confident athlete. "Hear that, Dad? She resolved the case. No more conflict of interest. Who's Lulu?"

Tabor cleared his throat. "There's more to it, Hannah." Retrieving a folder out of a black nylon briefcase, he handed it to his daughter. "Ms. Robbins was in the possession of a comprehensive media dossier spotlighting your life and the company's financials. A partner at her firm gave me a copy this morning." He turned to Camille. "It's quite impressive in scope, A-plus for execution."

"I didn't make that file, Mr. Tabor," Camille asserted, but the Gowear founder cut her off.

"Then you must have paid a fortune for it." He gave her a hard look, and then turned to Hannah who was flipping silently through the pages. His eyes softened. "It's really extensive, honey. Not only does it have our sales projections for the next five years, but the salaries of our senior executive team and stock vesting schedules." He shook his head. "And the stuff on you? It goes back even before you went to college. Someone found it in the office Ms. Robbins was using. Unless she's denying that too."

"I don't deny it was in the office."

Hannah lifted her head and Camille could see the folder was open to a printout of an old newspaper clipping. Hannah placed a finger on a grainy photograph of two people sitting at a table.

"This is my mom. They took this picture the day I signed with Stanford. We went to Olive Garden afterward." She pushed her hair behind her ear and studied Camille. The light in her golden eyes had dimmed considerably. "Where did you even find this? Did you really pay someone?"

Camille took a step back. "No. There's actually a very simple explanation."

"Great." Hannah flicked her thumb through the many pages of the folder. "Because I'd love to hear it."

"Okay."

"Or I could tell her."

The cavalry arrived in the form of a tall doctor in a white coat. Melissa was standing in the doorway with Jenna. Behind them was Bree, holding the bag of Martina's Italian food, and wearing a wary smile. Jenna looked deeply chagrined.

At the sight of the Emergency Room doctor, Jason Tabor's whole demeanor changed. Straightening his body, he was immediately on alert.

"Dr. Hill, hello." He moved to shake Melissa's hand. "Thank you for taking such good care of my daughter when she first came in. You were really helpful getting information back to my wife and me."

"You're welcome, Mr. Tabor, I'm glad she's awake. Hi, Hannah."

"Hi," Hannah replied. She was clearly confused. "Are you my doctor?"

Melissa nodded. "I was when you were first admitted."

"Do you know when I can get out of here?"

Melissa shook her head. "Neurology has to sign off first. They may want to keep you overnight."

It was Jason Tabor's turn to be confused. "Is everything okay?" It dawned on Camille that he might be worried Melissa was bringing them bad news.

Melissa was quick to reassure him. "They're just going through routine steps to get Hannah cleared and out of here. I stopped by for another reason."

"Oh, why are you here?"

Melissa pointed to the folder in Hannah's lap. "To talk about that file."

"You know about the file?" Jason Tabor's voice registered surprise.

Melissa looked pointedly at Jenna. "Unfortunately."

"I'm so sorry, Mr. Tabor," Jenna started, and then was interrupted by a chipper voice in the doorway.

"Food's here." Stacey's teased blond ponytail was just visible above a stack of pizza boxes piled high with containers of salads and other side dishes. Bags of sundries dangled from both hands threatening to spill their contents to the floor. Her face and torso were completely obscured. Jason Tabor moved to help.

"Let me get that, darling."

He took the load from her arms and placed it on a vacant chair next to Hannah's bed. Stacey put the bags on top. She stood back and surveyed the bounty and then bit her lip.

"I hope ya'll are hungry."

Jason Tabor gave his wife an indulgent look and then pointed at the folder. "I'll tell you what, Dr. Hill. I'll let you tell me about this file, if you'll join us for dinner. We may have enough to feed the ward." He pulled Stacey into his arms. "My wife likes to go the extra mile." Stacey accepted the compliment by leaning up to kiss his rugged cheek.

"I can relate to that, Jason," Melissa smiled. "This is my wife, Jenna, and she's exactly the same way."

EPILOGUE

Eight Months Later

The black folder lay conspicuously on the coffee table, its synthetic casing in stark contrast to the natural wood. Camille gave it a fond glance as she moved across the living room and handed a clear, plastic page insert to Hannah.

"Thanks, baby." Hannah slipped a piece of newsprint inside the protective sheath. Sitting back on the couch, she admired the picture. Though not identified, Camille and Hannah were clearly visible in a *Washington Post* photograph among a group of women in the Capital Pride Parade. All on motorcycles they were called "Dykes on Bikes" and had the honor of leading the event. Hannah had participated ten years running. It had been Camille's first time.

"This one might be my favorite." Hannah inspected the article, smiling as she read. She picked up the folder and flipped past the section Jenna had compiled featuring her alone, and on to the section chronicling Camille and Hannah as a couple. Jenna was mostly responsible for this section as well. She'd swapped it out for the Gowear financials, which she'd shredded and made Melissa stuff into a hospital bin reserved for toxic waste. Jenna had presented Camille with the new clippings at Christmas. It was her way of making amends for her starring role in folder-gate, as it was now known. After six months of being nearly inseparable, Hannah and Camille had generated a surprising amount of press. The glossy tidbits had been primarily in local society rags, but Camille still got a rush seeing herself paired publicly with Hannah.

As the face of Gowear philanthropy, Hannah was invited to everything. They'd celebrated Camille's move back to DC in style. Picking and choosing from an endless array of cultural, social, and political functions, they'd enjoyed the finest the nation's capital had to offer. Hannah thumbed past pictures of them smiling inside the National Gallery of Art and on the roof at the John F. Kennedy Center, the Potomac River sparkling behind them in the sunset. It was the best homecoming anyone could have asked for.

Camille looked over Hannah's shoulder to examine the most recent addition. She and Hannah were the focal point of the picture. They were in the middle of a pack of cool motorcycle chicks, Camille seated behind Hannah on the bike, embracing her from behind. The photographer had captured a smile on Camille's face that said there was nowhere on the earth she'd rather be. It was the look of a woman in love. Hannah appeared impossibly cool. Sitting tall on the bike, she roared confidently down P Street as behind them crowds of people cheered.

"You look so happy." Hannah popped open the black folder and positioned the plastic insert over the hooks.

"I was happy. I am happy, really happy," Camille clarified and kissed her girlfriend on the neck. She looked back at the photo. It had been a great day. Later, they'd hosted a raucous party at the Dupont Circle townhouse. Cory had come out from California and stayed in the guest room. Bonnie had brought her new girlfriend. Jenna had made a seven-layer dip.

Camille had moved in with Hannah two months ago, the day she'd formally moved back to DC and began working as a partner at Walker and Jenkins. By then both Mia and Lillian had left the firm. Mia having taken the job at Gowear and Lillian a position Mia had secured for her at another firm. It was a good career move for both women. Jenna heard through the office grapevine that Lillian had given the ring back. Camille wasn't sure what happened but something told her Mia's fear of commitment was to blame. Some things never change.

For six months Camille and Hannah had tried a bicoastal relationship. The practical side of Camille had needed to be sure. Yes, they had toe-curling sex, but was that all there was to it? In the end, she'd stopped questioning it. Didn't she already know the answer? The anticipation that built inside her each time she was set to see Hannah was the final giveaway. It didn't matter if it'd been an hour or a week. Tingles started in her lower abdomen and spread out until her entire body was affected. Her brain bore the biggest impact. Once Camille began thinking about Hannah, she couldn't stop until she was back in her arms.

For a couple who lived on opposite coasts, they'd logged an impressive amount of time together. It was amazing how small the world got when you paired raging libidos with access to private jets. They'd spent most weekends and all of the holidays together. At Christmas they'd shuttled between Jason Tabor's mansion in Great Falls, Virginia and Camille's childhood home in Woodley Park. Getting to know each other's fathers had been surprisingly fun. Both men seemed to be genuinely pleased that their daughters had found someone who made them happy. Joe Robbins was thrilled to have Camille close by. Jason Tabor had mentioned grandchildren. Stacey wanted to buy Camille an Audi.

Joe Robbins was now fully healed and teaching again. Back upstairs in the master bedroom, Hannah and Camille suspected he sometimes entertained company beyond the Kardashians. The day after his physical therapy ended he'd asked Martina to dinner and they'd been quietly dating ever since. Camille was happy for her father. Being in love was a glorious thing. It colored every day with happiness. Each morning you woke up and remembered you'd won the lottery.

Camille kissed Hannah on the neck then let her hands slip down to cup her breasts. "God, you feel good."

Hannah swatted her away. "Let me finish this. Then you can feel me as good as you want." Eight months of constant sex had not quelled their appetite for each other. If anything, they'd grown bolder in their play, more passionate. Hannah inserted the Capital Pride article and snapped the binder closed again. Returning it to the coffee table, she turned eagerly back to Camille, who was now walking toward the kitchen.

"Come back here," she demanded, pretending to pout. "It's not polite to get a girl all worked up and then leave her hanging."

Camille changed direction. It was not a request she could ignore. She walked around the couch, and guided Hannah down onto the cushions. Lying firmly on top of her, she slid a thigh between her legs.

"I'm so sorry," she said and brushed her lips against Hannah's. Pulling back a fraction of an inch, she whispered questions into her lips. "Will you forgive me? Can I make it up to you? Will you love me forever?"

"Yes," Hannah answered before capturing her mouth in a resolute kiss. "All of the above, yes."

Bella Books, Inc.

Women. Books. Even Better Together.

P.O. Box 10543
Tallahassee, FL 32302

Phone: 800-729-4992
www.bellabooks.com

CPSIA information can be obtained
at www.ICGtesting.com
Printed in the USA
LVHW010822170120
643905LV00002B/3